MAISY GROVE WEDDINGS

The ART of MOVING on

JESSICA MADDEN

ISBN: 978-0-646-72023-4

For those who struggle to move on and to find a place in this world,
you got this

Chapter 1

Emma

People say the pain gets easier as time goes by. But honestly, the pain feels worse every day without Dean.

I keep thinking to myself, what would happen if Dean didn't go down that road and went a different way? Would we not have been in the accident? I don't know, but it's too hard to think about. Every time a memory of him flashes across my mind, my heart crumbles further and further to dust.

Life didn't matter to me anymore after Dean had passed away, let alone my future. A drunk driver. And with one who couldn't have picked a better time than the night of our high school formal, I just didn't care about my HSC when I had to take them a few weeks later, which I ended up skipping. It wasn't like the HSC mattered. I wasn't going to attend university. Even if I was to take it, I couldn't study. I couldn't concentrate on anything.

I didn't go to the courts or find out the name of the man behind the wheel, but he was sent to jail for eighteen months for reckless driving and manslaughter. Eighteen months was way too short. He deserved a longer sentence.

After a couple of months, I moved out of my home. I couldn't live in Middleton anymore. Too many memories that I doubt would help me to move on. But that's the thing. I didn't want to move on. Moving on meant forgetting Dean, and I couldn't have that. At the same time, I didn't want to be around Middleton and have everyone pity me because I had lost my boyfriend.

So, I moved to Maisy Grove, a small town in the country, about an hour from Middleton. It was the perfect place for me to make a new start. I got a part-time job at this pie shop. There I help with making both savoury and sweet pies. I also serve the customers. And really, I love the job. Baking helps keep my mind off Dean.

In my spare time, I assist an elderly lady, Annie, on her farm. She lives on her own after her late husband passed away a few years ago. On the weekends I go with her to sell her jams and goat soap at the farmer's market. She runs riding lessons with her horses a few times a week also. I do what I can around the farm, feeding animals, and what I like the most is helping take care of her horses. Being around them makes me feel calm and puts the thought of that night out of my mind.

When I arrived in Maisy Grove, I had no idea where I was going to live, nor did I know where I was going to work. I just knew that this was the place I wanted to be to start a new chapter in my life. My parents had given me some money to help me get started. I found an ad in the newspaper from Annie, wanting to rent out her guest house at the back of her property. I told her I really needed a place to stay, though I didn't have a job yet. She allowed me to move into her furnished guest house, and in two days, I managed to get a job so I could start paying rent.

Being out here in the country is peaceful, and I'm glad to have been able to make this cosy town my home.

It's a nice, warm spring afternoon, and I have just finished my shift at the pie shop. I think of maybe going down to the river that runs by the farm for a quick dip. There is still a good few hours of daylight left.

As I pull up to the guest house, however, I see my brother's black sedan parked up front. What was he doing here? He knows I never like him coming around unannounced. Even if he is just here to check up on me, still I wanted him to let me know he is visiting. Not show up whenever he wanted. As I lock my door, I hear his voice travelling from the direction of the chicken coop, talking to Annie. I see his blond head as I approach them. Annie is scattering feed while the chickens strut around her feet, pecking at the ground for their food.

She catches my eye as I stroll over to them. "Oh, here she is. Hello, Emma. How was your day at work?"

I smile at her. "Hi, Annie. It was good." I turn to my brother. "Hey, Daniel. What are you doing here?"

Daniel walks out of the chicken coop towards me. "I'm sorry to come by. I just needed to talk to you about the wedding."

I frown. I love that my older brother is getting married to his girlfriend Kristy in a month's time, but I don't want to come to the wedding. I haven't kept in touch much with friends and family since I moved to Maisy Grove, but Daniel still tries to make sure we stay in contact. I don't even talk much to my parents. Occasionally I would call them up and let them know everything is alright, but then I would completely ghost them. It's not like I don't like anyone, it's just that I don't want to talk with anyone on what happened.

Months ago, Daniel invited me to his wedding, and my soon-to-be sister-in-law asked me to be one of her bridesmaids. I didn't want to at first, but Mum suggested that it would be good for me. So now I'm part of it.

Annie moves out of the chicken coop. "I'll let you guys talk. I'm going to get dinner ready."

When Annie is out of earshot, I turn back to my brother. "How is all of the wedding planning coming along?"

"It's good," he says. "We pretty much have everything ready to go. Next Monday afternoon we're doing a food tasting to choose our meals at the wedding."

I smile. "Nice."

"Are you able to come to Middleton tomorrow morning? Kristy is taking the bridesmaids to get their dresses fitted. You didn't come shopping for a dress last time, but Kristy really needs you to be there and try on your dress."

I nod, knowing that even if I wanted to say no, it was still required that I show up for it. "Sure, I can come. I'm sure my boss will be okay with it."

Daniel smiles. "Great. I'll let Kristy know. Also, Mum asked if maybe you would like to stay for dinner?"

When I left Middleton two years ago, I pretty much left everyone I know behind. I barely talk with my friends, Sammy and Katie, anymore. Occasionally I do let them know how I'm going through social media, but we aren't the close friends we used to be. I often find messages in my inbox, or sometimes they text me to ask how I'm doing or let me know they are thinking about me. It's mostly all small talk with them now. After Dean died, I just wanted to be left alone. Back then, I hardly told anyone how I was coping, but I feel that since moving away, the space has helped me a little, even though the hole in my heart is still there.

I especially don't talk much with my parents. I don't mean to do it. I just don't want them to constantly worry about how I'm doing or wonder if I'm coping with life okay. Each day is hard to get by, but I'm doing fine.

"I don't know," I answer. "I will see."

Daniel sighs like he knows it means I wasn't going to stay. "Come on, Emma. One dinner won't hurt."

"I'll see how I feel after the fitting. If I'm not too tired, I'll stay."

Daniel nods. "Alright then. I might see you tomorrow. I'll get Kristy to text you the location."

"Thanks, Daniel."

He gives me a hug before getting back into his car. I watch as he drives down the gravel driveway, the pit in my stomach growing the further he is from sight.

Once he's gone, I head inside my own place and take a shower before heading over to Annie's. I always have dinner with her so she doesn't have to be alone. Just as I enter, her blue cattle dog, comes running from the kitchen, barking when she knows it's me.

"Hey, girl. How you doing today?" I kneel down to scratch behind her ear.

Jessie licks my face in greeting before moving backwards, barking happily in response.

"That's good to hear, Jessie."

I get up and walk into the kitchen, Jessie following at my feet.

"Mmm, smells good," I tell her.

Annie looks up at me. "Oh thanks, dear. It's chicken and pasta."

My stomach grumbles at the mention. "Yum."

While Annie cooks, I set the table, placing down the placemats, along with the cutlery and drinks.

"How was your day, Emma?" Annie asks.

"It was good, thank you," I answer. Jessie walks over to her food bowl and stuffs her face. "You?"

"It has been lovely, dear."

I stand beside Annie at the stove, watching her stir the pasta with the chicken in the pot. Her short grey hair is pulled into a messy ponytail as she slumps over the stove.

"Do you need any help with cooking?" I ask.

Annie shakes her head, looking over at the set table before turning to me. "The pasta is almost done. How about you put together a garden salad?"

I do what she asks me, and go to the fridge, grab a packet of mixed leaf salad, tomatoes, a cucumber and red onion, then bring them to the island. I place the mixed leaf salad into a bowl and then chop the other ingredients into it. I leave the onion to last, hating the fact that cutting them always made me cry.

I sniff, wiping my eyes.

"Are you alright, Emma?" Annie asks.

"Yeah, I'm fine. Just the onion."

I put the sliced onion pieces into the salad, then grab a French dressing and drizzle it into the salad before giving the salad a good toss. When I'm done, Annie is serving the food onto our plates. I place the salad in the centre of the table and take my seat.

As Annie sits across from me, Jessie comes bounding over to the table and sits herself next to Annie, watching her with a wagging tail, probably hoping to score some of our meal.

"Your brother was telling me about his wedding next month," Annie says. "I remember when you first told me about it. I can't believe it has been six months already! The time surely goes quick."

I can't believe how much time has passed either. I was more surprised when Kristy asked me to be one of her bridesmaids. I almost said no, but then Daniel told me to take the opportunity.

"It definitely did go fast," I agree. "I'm meeting up with Kristy tomorrow to do a fitting for my dress."

"That is fine," Annie says, scooping a spoonful of pasta onto her fork. "What time do you need to meet her?"

"I think near noon."

"Okay. Tomorrow morning I have a new farmhand starting. Maybe you could show him a few things around the stables before you leave?"

I smile at Annie. She has a few farmhands who come in each day to help with taking care of the horses and the other animals, and there are two women who instruct riding lessons and sometimes give a hand around the stables when there are no students. "Sure. I can do that for you."

"Thank you, dear."

We eat in silence for a few minutes before Annie speaks again.

"Are you seeing your family tomorrow once you do the dress fitting?"

I shrug. "I don't know. The dress fitting isn't in Middleton, but my brother wants me to come to dinner at my parents' place before I head home..."

"But you don't want to."

I nod, staring at my food. Annie knows it all. My darkest thoughts, my deepest grief. She is always there to listen without judgement or overwhelming pity.

"Emma, dear, can I tell you something?" she asks.

I look up at her. "Of course."

"You should visit your parents. No matter what memories arise when you're there, visit them. I understand how hard it is to go back to a place where you have lost someone, but your parents are the most important people in your life, and you never know when it's your last time with them."

Annie is right. I shouldn't stop seeing my parents because of Middleton.

"Annie, was it hard for you when your husband died?" I asked. "Especially living here in this house?"

Annie continues chewing her food for a moment, looking around the room before turning to me. "When Pierce died, it was hard for me to accept. Each day was a struggle to get through, and sometimes, I didn't know how I was going to get through the day without him. But eventually you tell yourself 'I don't want to grieve anymore', and you do your best to move on. I can relate a lot to how you feel about Dean, and trust me when I say that as time goes by, you will heal and you will be stronger."

I shake my head. "It doesn't feel like I will ever heal. Since he died, I have this hole in my heart, and I don't think it's ever going to mend. Everyone tells me it will get easier, and the pain will ease, but it doesn't feel like it has."

"It may feel like that at first, Emma, but sometimes it takes longer to heal. When the time is right, you will be able to move on."

I nod slowly, trying to process what Annie is saying. It has been two years, and I still haven't been able to get over my boyfriend, even if we weren't together for so long. But at times it feels like we were together for a long time. Each day I tell myself that everything is going to be okay, but then something reminds me of Dean, and my heart breaks all over again. I don't know how I am going to move on. Maybe returning to Middleton to see my parents will help with moving on – like a final bit of closure.

But if I move on, will I end up forgetting Dean?

Chapter 2

Beck

What if people in Maisy Grove finds out what I did? What if nobody wanted me to be in this town?

I push these thoughts out of my head as I stare out the window of Mum's car as we drive past pastures and vineyards. People in Middleton may not have treated me nicely while I was in jail. The hate letters haven't stopped since. But I shouldn't worry because Maisy Grove is far away from Middleton, and no one will know me. I'll be fine.

"Don't worry too much about anyone," Mum assures me, like she was reading my mind. "You just concentrate on your work."

"I'll try." I turn to her. "I'm sorry you have to drive me back and forth to this place."

"Don't apologise. It's all good, Beck."

"Yeah, but it isn't fair to you. It won't be a year until I can drive again. I'll see if I can get a place near the farm so you don't have to worry about driving me."

"Honestly, Beck, it's fine. I'm just happy you are able to find something. I think this job will help you to fix up your life and start over."

"You think so?"

She smiles at me before turning her eyes back to the road. "I think so."

"Have you told Dad about the job?"

Mum doesn't say anything at first. "Your father doesn't have to know anything."

"Has he been treating you right while I was gone?"

Mum doesn't answer as she pulls into a gravel driveway, welcomed by a sign that says Maisy Grove Stables.

"Let's not worry about that right now," she says. "We're here."

Of course she uses our arrival as the excuse to end the conversation, but I got my answer. Hopefully once I start earning enough money, I can get a place and Mum can move in with me. It's about time she leaves that jerk behind.

I stare out at the modern yellow farmhouse. To its left are fences to a field, surrounding the stables. Two brown horses graze in the field, looking as peaceful as I dream to be.

"This is a lovely place," Mum says, shifting the gear into park and switching off the ignition. She then turns to me. "I think you're going to like it here, Beck."

I scoff. "I don't know, Mum. Shovelling horse manure is not something I want to be doing every day."

"Just look at this place and how they hired you, despite your record. Now, go and start your day. I will be back later to pick you up."

"Thanks for the lift. I'll see you later."

Mum waits until I walk up the stairs before she turns the ignition back on and does a U-turn, heading back down the driveway.

The air definitely smells like horse manure. I'm not sure how I'm going to be able to work here when I have to hold my breath all the time.

No one answers when I knock on the front door, so I decide to walk over to the stables to see if Annie, my new boss, is inside. There are a couple of horses inside, but still no people until I spot a blonde woman in one of the stalls, grooming a golden coated horse with a white mane.

"I have to go out today, Blondie, but I'll try to come back early so we can spend some time together," the woman says, a brush in one hand as she combs through the coat, her other hand on the horse's snout.

The horse neighs in response.

"Yes, I know we go riding on my day off, but today we can't. Hopefully we can go out for a ride later today. How does that sound?"

Blondie neighs.

"That's a good girl."

I approach the stall. "Excuse me?" She turns to me, her blue eyes narrowing slightly, her gaze holds a hint of curiosity, as if sizing me up without quite meaning to. Her hair is pulled back into a ponytail, where she wore jeans and a pink plaid shirt. "Hi, are you Annie?"

She shook her head. "Annie should be inside the house."

"I just came from the house and no one answered."

The woman thinks for a second. "She could be around the back with the chickens and goats."

She puts the brush down and then opens the door, locking it behind her. Gesturing me the direction, we started walking alongside each other, exiting the stables and out onto the gravel driveway.

"You must be Beck, right?" The woman asks me. "You're the new farmhand?"

"That's me."

"Nice to meet you, Beck. I'm Emma."

Emma leads me behind the house towards a chicken coop and goat pen.

"Are you a farmhand too?"

She shakes her head. "No, I rent the guest house." She points to a small house opposite the chickens and goats that look like a cottage. "Sometimes when I don't have work, I help Annie out on the farm."

"Cool."

We round the corner to see a bunch of goats surrounding an elderly lady scattering food from a bucket on the ground. One goat, a black one, tries to steal the bucket.

"Shadow," she scolds the goat. "Wait your turn."

"Annie," Emma calls out as she leans up on the fence.

Annie looks up and smiles at us before making her way through the goats and over to us.

"This is Beck," Emma tells her. "The new farmhand."

Annie holds her hand out to me, and I shake it. "Beck, hello. It's nice to meet you. I'm Annie."

I greet her. "It's a pleasure to meet you."

"Annie, I'm just going to finish up with Blondie, and then I'm going to head out," Emma says.

"Alright, dear," Annie says. "You go finish your task. I'm going to give Beck a tour of the place, and then can you show him around the stables before you leave?"

Emma smiles. "Okay." She strolls back to the stables.

Annie comes through the gate to be at my side. "It's good to meet you, Beck. I'm happy to have you here."

"Thank you for hiring me. I know you probably wouldn't want a criminal for working for you, but I –"

Annie signals for me to stop. "I have read your record, and I'm not here to judge you. I hired you because I believe this place will help you to turn your life around."

I smile at her. When I spoke to Annie on the phone about the job, she was very understanding after I told her about my trouble past. I needed more people like her in my life.

"Are there any questions you would like to ask?"

I look around at my surroundings before turning back to her. "What will be my role here?"

"Like I mentioned on the phone, you will be helping with feeding the animals and cleaning out their pens. Here on the farm, I have chickens, goats and horses. During the week, I have two ladies – Darcy and Roxanne – who come in to help out with the horses. They may help you with mucking out the stalls, but mostly they will be taking care of the horses. In the afternoon, they instruct riding lessons, as well as on the weekends."

"Do I need to help out with the riding lessons?"

"No, you don't need to help out unless Darcy or Roxanne needs an assistant."

"What about Emma? She told me she helps out around here."

Annie nods. "Yes, Emma occasionally helps out with the horses. She's especially fond of Blondie. You'll often see her hanging around her stall. Sometimes she takes Blondie for rides. Now, let me show you around the farm, and then I'll let you get started with your work."

We head towards the stables.

"You'll be starting at 6 am seven days a week and you'll finish around 6 pm," Annie continues. "On Saturdays, I go to the farmer's market, where I sell goat's soap and jams. Emma also helps me, and you're welcome to tag along. How far away do you live, Beck?"

"I live about an hour from here."

Annie rubs her chin. "That seems pretty far for you to get here, especially when you can't drive. How did you get here this morning?"

"My mum drove me. I'm thinking of maybe renting a place in town so I don't have to drive so far each day."

"No need for you to rent a place in town. The last farmhand I had rented out one of the bedrooms in my house. It's a master bedroom that has its own bathroom, as well as a living space. The kitchen, of course, you share with me. I think it's something you'll like."

It sounds perfect. At least I won't have to live with my best friend Chandler and his girlfriend anymore. They could have their privacy back. And Mum and I won't constantly have to take the trip down here. It'll definitely be easier on both Mum and me.

I especially don't have to worry about running into my father around Middleton. I'm safer here in Maisy Grove than I am in my hometown.

"That will be totally great, Annie," I say. "Thank you very much for that."

"You're welcome. But if you feel like the place isn't so great for you, I understand. I'm not going to make you stay. Maybe you'll be able to find something around Maisy Grove."

"That's one of the plans."

Just then, a barking blue cattle dog comes running over to us.

"That's Jessie," Annie says. "If you need help gathering up the animals, Jessie is great at making sure the animals all come together."

I kneel down and scratch the dog behind the ears. "Hello, Jessie."

Jessie sticks out her tongue as her tail wags.

Standing back up, Annie and I walk through the stables with Jessie at our heels. Annie shows me around, giving me a rundown on what my duties are going to be. There are a lot, and I'm honestly not sure how I'm going to be able to get everything done in a day.

But my mum is right. This is a place I'm going to enjoy, even if it isn't such a great job.

Chapter 3

Emma

Kristy was like a sibling to me. After Dean died, when I wasn't with my friends, she would take me out, try to cheer me up. We would get our hair and nails done, sometimes we would have lunch or even have a spa day. I appreciated all of the things she did to try to get me to feel better, but most of the days when I was with her, I just wanted to be in my room. Alone.

Since moving to Maisy Grove, I haven't seen much of her. But she drove out here once and took me out to lunch. It was a week after she and Daniel had gotten engaged. That was when she had asked me to be one of her bridesmaids. I really didn't want to be a part of the wedding, but at the same time, I couldn't say no to her. Not after all of the things she has done for me.

When I pull up at the front of the bridal shop, Kristy is waiting outside, along with her friends, Sandra and Tracey. Sandra is the maid of honour, while Tracey is also a bridesmaid.

As I'm getting out of the car, my phone rings. I dig it out of my handbag and see Dean's mother's name across my screen. My heart sinks when I see her name. Every now and again his mother calls me to see how I am doing. Only I ignore Adeline Myers' calls, even her text messages. I'm afraid if I answer the phone, I will choke up. I don't want to talk to either of his parents, because they only remind me of my boyfriend. Especially his dad.

Declining the call, I step out of the car. Kristy smiles at me as I stroll over to them.

"It's so great to see you, Emma," she greets me.

I return the smile and hug her. "It's great to see you too."

"How have you been? It feels like I haven't seen you in a while."

"It has been a while. I haven't seen you since May, when we went shopping for the dresses. Are you doing a fitting for your dress as well?"

Kristy nods. "Yes, I am. But we're going to do you girls first before I try on my dress. After the fitting, the three of us are going out to lunch. Would you like to join us?"

I glance over Kristy's shoulder at Sandra and Tracey. I didn't know Kristy's friends all that well, and I didn't feel comfortable with them around. But since Daniel wants me to stay and see our parents later, I might as well stay for lunch.

I smile. "I'll be happy to."

The four of us head inside. Francesca, a middle-aged Italian woman, greets us with a smile.

We follow her upstairs to where the bridesmaid dresses are. She gets us to sit in a corner where there are some seats that surround a change room and a mirror.

Sandra is the first to get up and try on her dress, and just a few moments later, she emerges from the dressing, wowing us with how well the blue compliments her tone. At first, I wasn't so keen on the sleeveless A-line scoop dress, but seeing it on Sandra, it's definitely the right choice to wear. I especially love the high-low layered chiffon skirt. And the colour is just spectacular.

Tracey is next. As we wait for her to try it on, I try not to let my thoughts drift. But how could I not? The last time I was excited to get all dressed up was for our formal. If Dean were here, he would be coming with me to the wedding. I can imagine him seeing me in it for the first time; his eyes widening, his lips parting slightly. I shake my head and watch as Tracey makes her way out of the change room, and is just as spectacular in the dress. The colour looks really great against her dark skin.

Then it's my turn. I put the dress on and as I stare at my reflection, I can definitely picture Dean loving this dress on me. The thought brings the sting of tears to my eyes. Not now. I can't cry. This dress fitting should be about Kristy.

"Everything okay in there, Emma?" Francesca asks.

I wipe my eyes, trying to collect myself. "Yeah, I'm okay."

I move the curtain and emerge, swirling in the dress as I show it off to the others. The dress makes me feel like a princess attending a ball.

"The dresses really look great!" Kristy says. "I'm so happy with how they all came out."

Francesca claps her hands together. "Perfect." She turns to me. "Get changed, and I'll take the dresses. Then we'll go downstairs, and Kristy can try on her dress."

I do as she says. As we head downstairs, Kristy walks alongside me.

"Are you okay, Emma?"

I nod, hoping my eyes aren't showing the sting I'm still feeling. "I'm okay."

Kristy arches her eyebrow, like she couldn't believe me a second. "Are you sure? I can't help but sense that trying on that dress didn't make you happy. Are you happy with the dress?"

I smile at Kristy. "Of course I am. The dress is lovely."

Kristy grasps my arm gently. "You're happy with the dress, but not completely happy?"

I stand there, staring into her hazel eyes. That's what I like about Kristy. We aren't blood related, but I consider her my sister. She could always see right through me when something was wrong. Like at one time when Dean and I first started dating, I thought he was already cheating on me after a month of being together. I went out shopping with Mum, and I saw him sitting at the food court with a girl. He claimed she was his cousin. I didn't believe him. Kristy knew something was wrong as soon as she sat down to join my family for dinner that night. She told me to hear him out, and that maybe I was jumping to conclusions, that maybe Dean was telling the truth. If he wasn't, then I had the choice to leave. I called Dean later that night, and surprisingly he answered. We talked, and I apologised to him for jumping to conclusions and accusing him for cheating. He forgave me.

"I wish Dean could be here and see me in this dress," I tell her.

Kristy gives me a small smile. "He would have loved you in that dress."

"Kristy, Emma, are you guys coming?" Tracey asks us.

Kristy turns to her and nods.

Before we follow Tracey, Kristy turns back to me. "We can talk later, okay?"

I nod. "Okay."

We join the others in front of a change room and mirror. Francesca comes over with a garment bag.

"Are you ready?" Francesca smiles at Kristy.

"Ready."

She disappears into the change room with Francesca. A few minutes later, Kristy emerges in the most stunning dress I've ever seen, and I can just imagine my brother's face when he sees her walking down the aisle in it. Her A-line dress is strapless with a sweetheart neckline and floral designs around her torso that flow down to the waistline. She looks absolutely gorgeous in it.

"What do you guys think?" Kristy asks, staring at her reflection in the mirror before swirling around to face us.

"Amazing," Sandra says. "You look gorgeous in it."

"The dress is stunning," Tracey adds.

Kristy smiles at her friends before turning to me, waiting for my opinion.

"My brother is going to be knocked off his feet when he sees you in it." I give her a small smile.

Kristy's smile widens as she turns back to the mirror, unable to take her eyes off the dress. She runs her hands over the material.

"The dress is beautiful," she tells Francesca. "It looks even more amazing than when I first tried it on."

Francesca smiles. "Perfect. Do you have any concerns about the dress? Nothing needs to be altered?"

Kristy shakes her head, turning to Francesca. "No. Everything is perfect. Thank you very much."

After Kristy gets changed out of the dress and Francesca takes it and puts it in the garment bag, we then head over to the cashier to settle everything. There's also a card around the hanger to tell which dress is which. I take mine, and the four of us thank Francesca one last time before heading out to our cars.

"Thank you, girls, for coming along today," Kristy tells us. "I really appreciate it."

"I can't wait for the wedding," Tracey says. "I can't believe it's in a month."

"I know. I can't either. It's all happening so fast!" Kristy turns to me. "Emma, do you still want to come to lunch with us?"

I nod. I might as well, because if I don't, my brother is probably going to ask me why I didn't. I'm still not sure about going to see my parents. I really don't feel like staying here for the rest of the day. This place holds many memories. Ones I just want to forget.

Kristy smiles. "Okay, well let's get going then."

After lunch, Kristy says goodbye to her friends, leaving just the two of us in the car park. It's a little after one o'clock, and all I can think about is getting back to the farm. All I want to do is head home, maybe take Blondie for a ride if she isn't being used for Darcy's and Roxanne's riding lessons this afternoon. It's also warm out, maybe I could squeeze in a dip down at the river if I made it back in time

"How are you feeling?" Kristy asks me. "Are you okay from earlier?"

I nod. I'm never going to be okay, but I don't want to mention this to Kristy. "I'm okay."

"That's good. How have you been lately?" She looks at me with concern.

I lean up against my car. "I've been alright. I'm getting by."

She chews her bottom lip, like she was thinking of how she will say her next words. "Daniel was telling me the guy who had hit you guys was released from jail a few weeks ago."

My heart sinks deeply in my chest from the news. Since Dean's death, I haven't kept up with the courts. I have no idea what happened to the other driver, other than what his parents have told me. The driver was sentenced to jail for eighteen months for manslaughter. He was also charged with driving under the influence.

I probably would have heard about his release from Dean's parents just like before. Then I think of the call I had from his mother earlier. If I had answered, is this the news she would tell me?

"The driver is out of jail?" I say.

I don't even know the driver's name. If anyone had once told me, I probably wasn't paying any attention. Now, the thought of him being back on the streets sends chills down my spine. I don't even know what this guy looks like, so I'm sure if I were to bump into him on the street, I wouldn't know it was him. Even if I were to know who he was, how would I react when I see him?

Kristy nods. "Yeah, he is."

"Why didn't anyone tell me he was out?"

"I thought Daniel told you?"

I shake my head. "No, he didn't. Not even my parents."

Kristy turns her gaze from me. "Sorry. I didn't mean to tell you this. I thought you would have known." She forces herself to look back at me, but her eyes don't meet mine. "Maybe they didn't tell you because they were afraid of how you would react."

How would I react? How am I reacting? Angry? Sad? I don't know...

Instead of sticking around long enough to find out, I unlock my car. "I'm going to head home. Thank you for today, Kristy."

She gives me a small smile. "It's no problem at all. Daniel and I will let you know if there's any other wedding stuff coming up. It probably won't be until the week of the wedding with the bachelorette party and the wedding rehearsal."

"Okay." I open the car door.

"Are you coming to dinner tonight?"

I nod. "Yes, I'm coming."

Just as I close the door, Kristy stops it before it shuts. "Hey, I didn't mean to upset you."

"You didn't. I just wish someone had told me sooner instead of waiting to tell me."

"Right. Of course. See you later, Emma."

Kristy moves away from the car, and I close the door. I wave goodbye to my soon-to-be sister-in-law and pull out of the parking lot.

Chapter 4

Beck

It's after three, and I already feel dead. I'm sure as soon as my mother picks me up, I'll end up falling asleep in the car. I don't mind the job really, caring for the animals was fine. But mucking out the horse stalls? No, thank you! I'm one hundred per cent sure I smell like horse manure. How can these people do this all the time?

Wiping off the sweat on my forehead, I was finally done with moving the hay bales into the barn. Closing the doors, I went over to the goats and chickens to see if they need anything. Parents are starting to arrive now, dropping off their kids for lessons with Darcy and Roxanne. I decide to stay clear of the stables so as not to be in anyone's way. I'm sure the ladies have everything under control and don't need me at all.

I stand at the fence, watching the hens walk around, pecking at the ground when a black rooster struts in like an overprotective guardian. In the goat pen next door, the goats happily sit around, some chewing on the grass. This one brown male goat stands up from where he was sitting next to a black and white goat. He stares me down, looking ready to head butt me with his horns if I was to dare to come into the pen. I go to open the gate to check on the food supply, but barely make it in after a few steps. The goat comes charging at me, and I quickly escape before he rams me with his horns.

"What's your problem, mate?" I ask him as he stares down at me. "Can't I check on your food?"

"Having a stare down with Buckley?"

I look up and see Emma walking over to me with a beach bag over her shoulder. At her heels was Annie's dog, Jessie. At least Jessie was friendly and didn't hate me like Buckley.

I point at the goat. "That goat hates me."

Emma laughs as she stands beside me. Jessie makes her way in between us, and I bend down to pat her head, scratching behind her ears.

"Buckley doesn't like men," Emma explains. "Annie once told me that her husband or even her son couldn't get into the pen without Buckley coming after them. Even the last farmhand had problems. He is sweet on the ladies, though."

I stand up, letting out a small laugh. "Sweet on the ladies? Why is that?"

Emma shrugs. "I honestly don't know."

"You don't know? How am I supposed to clean the pen if he keeps charging at me?"

"You just have to try. Maybe try and distract him with something."

"Like what?"

"I don't know."

I sigh. "Great. Out of every animal on his farm, it's the goat that hates me."

Emma laughs. "I'm sure he'll get used to you eventually."

"Sure he will."

"What are you doing now? You look like you need to cool down."

"I don't know. I've done everything. Not sure if I should take a break for a bit."

Emma gestures to her bag. "I'm going for a swim."

I furrow my eyebrows. "Where are you going swimming?"

"There's a river nearby." She bites her lip and looks down at her feet before looking back at me. "You look exhausted. Why don't you take your break?... Maybe you would like to go for a swim?"

I open my mouth slightly, but don't answer straight away. I glance towards the farmhouse where Annie is. A quick dip definitely sounded nice, but would Annie allow me to go when I should be working? I was allowed two breaks, a thirty-minute lunch break and another short break.

"I'm working, Emma," I explain. "I don't think I'll be allowed to leave the property."

Emma shakes her head. "You aren't leaving the property. The river runs through it. Take a quick break. Or you can make it that you're walking Jessie. And if Annie asks about your whereabouts, I'll will take the blame."

"Thanks, Emma, but I don't want you to take the blame for me."

"Are you sure? I don't think Annie would want you to collapse from heatstroke. The animals have plenty of water and shelter to keep them cool, so they should be okay for a bit. Besides, I don't plan to stay down at the river for a long time. It would be nice to, but I have somewhere to be later."

I take another look at the house, then at the goats and chickens, before turning back to Emma. I nod. "Just a quick dip."

A swim will definitely be better than drinking a cold bottle of water.

Emma smiles, and then lead the way with Jessie walking alongside us. We leave the farm area and walk into a field behind the pasture for the horses, heading towards a tree line where Emma says is the river.

"So, Beck, what were you doing before you got his job?" Emma asks.

"I was working in a supermarket."

"And you gave that up to be a farmhand? A change of scenery, I suppose?"

I can't tell her the truth. If I do, she'll see me differently, maybe not even talk to me or would want to keep a clear distance. I definitely can't go around my hometown without people giving me dirty looks, knowing what I did two years ago. It was something I wasn't proud of, and if I could, I would redo everything again to make sure I wouldn't make that mistake.

I nod. "Yeah, change of scenery, I guess. It's something different for me. I mean, it's not so much of a great job, but I don't mind it. What do you do for work?"

"I work at a pie bakery," she answers.

"Oh, cool. Like savoury or sweet pies?"

"Both."

"Do you make them?"

Emma nods, pushing a strand of hair behind her ear. "I do. I also make apple pies to sell when I help Annie at the farmer's market on Saturdays. Just behind the guest house, we are growing a variety of berries to make her jams."

"Cool. I'm going to have to try her jam and your pies. What days do you work at the bakery?"

"Monday to Friday. Though this Friday I will be working to make up for taking a day off today."

"Well, I'll have to stop by some time and try some."

Jessie barks at something, running ahead of us. We are almost at the tree line.

"So, how long have you been living with Annie?" I ask.

"About a year and ten months. I like it out here. It's peaceful."

"Have you always lived in Maisy Grove?"

"No."

"Where did you used to live?"

We reach the tree line, and from there I see the river. Emma doesn't answer my question as she calls out for Jessie, who has disappeared behind the trees.

Emma turns to me. "Be careful around here. There could be snakes. Sometimes I worry about Jessie finding one and getting herself bitten."

I nod.

Jessie is just on the edge of the river now, staring at the water.

"Go on in, girl," Emma tells her.

Without hesitation, Jessie jumps into the water, barking happily.

Emma puts her bag down beside a tree. "Jessie loves swimming. Every time I come down here, she likes to follow me."

"I wouldn't blame her. On a day like today, swimming would be a great idea." I wipe the sweat from my forehead. "Gosh, if this spring weather is hot, what's summer going to be like?"

"Worse. The humidity is horrible."

Emma reaches for the hem of her shirt and pulls it over her head. My breath catches in my throat, taking in her floral bikini top. Next she slips off her shorts, and she has on matching bottoms. She has a nice figure, one that goes nicely with her swimsuit. I force myself to look away so she won't think I'm watching her.

Emma then races to the river, walking in, and when the water is at her thighs, she dives under. She is under the water for a second before resurfacing, pushing her hair back.

"Aren't you coming in?" she calls out.

I realise I have been busy staring at Emma to take off my own clothes. I take off my shirt, where I'm pretty sure I caught Emma blushing, probably taking a good look at my biceps and abs. I did a lot of working out in the last year. Next, I take off my jeans, only leaving on my boxers, which should be good enough to go swimming in.

The water felt like a refresher from the heat.

"This water feels so good," I say.

"It is," Emma replies. "I like coming down here to go for a swim. Sometimes, when I feel like I need to get away from the farm for a bit, I come down here. It's a place where I like to relax and think."

"Think about what?"

There's sadness in her eyes when I ask about it.

"Just stuff," she says without elaboration.

"Are you okay? Do you want to talk about something?"

"No. I'm fine."

She dips under the water. Jessie swims past me and jumps up onto the river bank, shaking the water out of her fur.

When Emma resurfaces, I say, "Are you sure you are fine? You seem sad about something."

The smile that was once on Emma's face turns to a frown. "Look, I invited you down here for a dip in the water to cool off. I didn't ask you to start questioning my life."

Her sudden change in mood surprises me, leaving me unsure whether I should take that as a hint that I'm no longer welcome here.

"I'm sorry," is all I can say.

I turn to get out of the water, but Emma is the one who beats me to it.

"Emma, I said I'm sorry," I apologise for the second time. "You don't need to leave."

Emma grabs a towel from her bag and wraps it around herself before stuffing her clothes in the bag and slipping on her shoes.

She turns to me. "Listen, I know I invited you down here, but forget about this place. I don't ever want to see you here."

Without another word, she calls Jessie and heads back for the farm.

I should probably head back too. I don't want to be gone for too long that Annie comes looking for me.

With nothing to dry myself with, I put my clothes back on. Even if they get wet, I'm sure the sun will dry it fairly quickly by the time I walk from here to the farm.

Chapter 5

Emma

The moment I walk inside the house, the guilt hits me. Why on earth did I yell at the new guy like I did? All because he had asked me something about my life? He was just getting to know me.

I change out of my bikini and dry myself before putting on my clothes again. It's just after 3:30. In a couple of hours, I'll make my way to my parents' place for dinner. The thought of going there already exhausts me. When I go, they'll probably ask how I'm going and what I'm doing, the same questions over and over again that I don't want to answer. No one wants to accept that I'm okay. They think I'm not telling the truth about how I'm really feeling, only because I don't want to discuss what happened to Dean.

I boil the jug and make myself a cup of tea. As I wait for the water to boil, I glance out the kitchen window that faces the back of Annie's house, the goats' pen and the chicken coop. Beck's out there, feeding the chickens. Buckley is watching him from his pen, ready to charge if Beck tries to come inside. The thought of that small goat trying to ambush Beck makes me laugh.

Damn it, Emma. Why did you yell at him for? He is probably going to be sticking around for a while as the new farmhand. I doubt he would want to be around someone like me, who yells at him at the first opportunity she has. All Beck was trying to do was make conversation, and I jumped down his neck for it. He'll probably be too afraid to speak to me ever again, even a simple "hello" will probably scare him off.

The jug stops boiling, and I pour the water into my mug, adding the milk and sugar.

There's a knock on my door as I stir my tea. Leaving the mug, I answer the door.

"Hey, Annie. What can I do for you?"

"Just checking up on you, dear. I heard you and Beck got into a little disagreement, all because he asked questions about you."

I move aside, gesturing Annie inside. She steps over the threshold and follows me into the kitchen, where I offer her a tea. She accepts my offer and sits down at the table while I make her a cup.

"I don't know why I snapped at him," I explain.

I set the cup down in front of her before sitting down across from her with my own. "I just don't do well when people ask me about my life. He especially asked me where I was from and what brought me to Maisy Grove. I can't answer those without having to think about Dean, and I don't want to have to explain it in full detail."

Annie gives me a small smile, reaching across the table and putting her hand over mine. "Then don't explain it. Tell Beck or anyone that you aren't ready to tell them the answers. When you are ready and feel comfortable explaining things, tell them, but you don't have to go into full detail of why you moved here. And maybe instead of thinking of the tragic, think of the happiest times you have had with Dean."

Annie was right, it's something I could do instead of snapping at people. Even when I was getting to know Annie when I first came here, I didn't exactly like having to tell her answers to questions I didn't want to answer, but I still did it. And maybe I wouldn't have a place to stay without doing so.

I nod. "I can do that."

Annie gives me an encouraging smile. "Don't forget to apologise to him. He was confused about what happened. Also, the next time you invite him down to the river or anywhere, make sure to check with me first. He works for me, okay? I want to know where he is, even during his breaks."

"Okay, Annie."

Annie drinks her tea, and for a moment, we sit there in silence.

"Are you still going to see your parents?" Annie asks me.

"Yeah, I am."

Annie drinks the last of her tea. "I hope you enjoy your time with your family. Remember, Emma, not to get upset every time someone mentions the past or something about Dean. We all go through our own demons, and moving on can be difficult. But that's the thing: life moves on. We can't live in the past forever. We have to keep moving forward, even when it's hard."

I take in her words as she gets up, walking over to the sink to rinse out her mug before placing it on the drying rack. I sit there with my hands on my mug, thinking of everything. Each day is a struggle for me. Maybe I was just eighteen and hadn't been with Dean for long, but he still meant the world to me. He was everything. I was in love with him, and even if he was the only guy I dated, I knew he was the one for me. I wanted to spend the rest of my life with him.

How do you move on from losing someone you love, someone who makes up your entire world?

I finish my tea and then rinse my mug in the sink, catching a glimpse of Beck outside my window, talking with the goats. Buckley is still staring him down, and all I can do is laugh. As I watch Beck, I can picture him down by the river as he pulls off his shirt, his muscles flexing when he does. I haven't looked at another man since losing Dean.

Did moving on mean finding someone else to fall in love with? The thought sends chills down my body. How can I think about falling for someone else? I don't think I could ever be capable of that.

I glance at the clock on the wall. There's plenty of time to bake.

Just like I was hoping it would, the pie finishes baking by the time I'm supposed to leave. Once the pie finishes cooling, I wrap it in foil before grabbing my handbag and heading out the door.

I search around the farm, hoping Beck's still around and hasn't finished work yet. There are a lot of cars around, parents coming to pick up their children from lessons. I see Darcy and Roxanne in the riding ring with three younger children and two teens.

Around to the barn, I check where the hay is stored, but Beck isn't there. So next I check the stables, and there he is, standing in front of Blondie's stall. The two of them alone in the stables.

Beck rubs her snout, talking to her softly.

"You know Emma pretty well, don't you?" he asks. "You don't think she'll stay mad at me for long, do you?"

Blondie neighs in response.

"Yeah, I hope you're right. I didn't mean to offend her. Maybe you should talk to her for me? Tell her not to get upset with me if I ask her questions?"

Blondie doesn't respond. I laugh softly, the guilt I had from earlier quickly disappearing.

"Getting the horse to do your job, huh?" I say as I walk towards him.

Beck turns to me, taking a step back from Blondie. He rubs a hand on the back of his neck. "Hey. How much did you hear?"

"Just you wanting Blondie to talk to me about not getting upset with you."

I stand close to him, the apple pie between us. Blondie watches both of us while Beck takes a step away from me.

"It's okay," I say. "I'm not going to get upset with you."

Beck lets out a sigh of relief.

"I'm sorry about before. I didn't mean to snap at you. I shouldn't have done that. I hope you can forgive me, and we can start over?"

Beck's lips curl into a smile. "Of course we can start over. And I promise I won't ask questions about your personal life again. Not until you're ready to tell me."

I return his smile. "Thank you for understanding." I hold out the pie to him. "I made this for you."

Beck takes the pie. "Thanks. I wasn't expecting an apology straight away. I figured I wouldn't see you until tomorrow."

"I felt bad the moment I walked into my house. And then Annie came in, we talked. I thought maybe I should bake a pie as an apology."

"You didn't have to bake me a pie just to say sorry."

"I know. But at least now it gives you a chance to try one."

"Well, thanks again. I'll definitely have some tonight for dessert."

"I need to go, so I guess I will see you tomorrow."

"Of course. See you, Emma."

I turn to Blondie, and pat her snout with one hand while rubbing her neck with the other. "You keep an eye on Beck for me, okay?"

Blondie snorts.

"I'll see you tomorrow. Maybe we'll go for a ride. How does that sound?"

Blondie neighs.

I smile at her and say goodbye before leaving. I glance over my shoulder at Beck and catch his eyes still on me, making my heart race at the sudden attention. As I get into my car, I see Annie standing on her front veranda, watching me. I wave a goodbye, and she waves back, soundless, but as if she has something to say.

Daniel and Kristy are already at my parents' place when I arrive. I wish I could get back in my car and be anywhere but here. It's not that I don't want to have dinner with my parents or see them again, because I do. I'm just not sure how things will turn out tonight. Especially considering what Kristy had told me earlier. How can I face my family knowing that they're hiding a secret from me? How could they not tell me that he was released from jail a few weeks ago? I deserve the right to know that man is roaming the streets again. Although I may never come across him, I still have the right to know that he is out there. Then again, I have been declining Dean's mother's calls.

Mum opens the door before I have the chance to turn back. She greets me with a wide smile and open arms. "Emma, it's so good to see you."

I hug my mother. "It's so good to see you too, Mum."

"How have you been?"

I pull away from her. "I'm doing well."

"Come on in, sweetie."

Mum moves aside for me to enter, closing the door behind her. She then leads me to the dining room, where everyone is. Kristy is setting the table while Daniel is pouring everyone some fruit juice. Dad places a bowl of garden salad in the centre of the table.

"Hey, everyone," I say.

Everyone looks up, and Dad is the first to walk over to me.

"Hey, sweetie." He pulls me into a hug. "It's so good to see you. Have a seat. Dinner is almost ready."

Mum and Dad leave for the kitchen. Daniel kisses Kristy, telling her that he'll be back in a second before turning to me, giving me a pat on the shoulder.

"I'm glad you decided to come, Emma."

I give my brother a warm smile.

Daniel leaves the dining room, leaving just Kristy and me. I walk over to the table, resting my hands on one of the chairs. Kristy looks over her shoulder towards the kitchen before turning to me.

"I wasn't sure if you were coming or not after what I said earlier," she says.

I give her a smile. "It's not what you said. Let's put aside what you said earlier. It doesn't mattery anyway. I don't know who the guy is, so it's not like I'll ever come across him on the street."

Kristy doesn't say a word, but she continues to look up at me with her considerate eyes.

"Still," I continue, "I wish someone had informed me, but thank you for telling me, even if no one in my family did. Also, we both know that if I didn't show, Daniel would try and convince me to come again, or one of my parents would try to put together something to force me."

"Well, thank you for coming. I miss having you around." Kristy gives me a small smile, and I return it.

Mum and Dad return with a plate of steaks and a bowl of mashed potatoes. Mum places a steak on everyone's plate while Dad puts the bowl next to the salad.

I take a seat across from Kristy. "Dinner smells delicious, Mum."

"Thank you, sweetie," Mum smiles, then disappears back to the kitchen again.

Dad sits down at the head of the table between Kristy and me, and when Daniel returns, he takes the seat next to Kristy.

"What has been happening, Emma?" Dad asks. "Anything new?"

Here come the questions. I reach for my glass of apple juice. "Nothing interesting." I sip my drink.

"Come on, Em. Something should be happening in your life."

I place my glass down. "Nope, it hasn't."

Mum returns with a plate of dinner rolls and places it in the centre of the table.

We dig into the food. For a moment, no one speaks until all our plates are full.

"How's the wedding planning coming along, you two?" Mum asks my brother and Kristy.

"Good," Daniel says. "The girls had their dress fittings today. Next Monday Kristy and I have food tastings. Everything for the wedding is coming along well."

"That's great to hear."

We are back to being silent again. After a few minutes, Dad speaks.

"Emma, your mother and I know you don't watch or read the news..." My chest tightens, and I already know what's coming before Dad says it. "We not only invited you to dinner to catch up with you, but we also wanted to inform you that—"

"He got out of jail two weeks ago," I say before he completes the sentence. Dad looks at me with confusion, probably wondering how I had known. So I add, "Kristy let it slip today."

"Honey, we want you to know that if you need to talk about anything, we're here," Mum says.

I put my cutlery down, suddenly in no mood to eat. "And talk about what? Dean? The accident? The man who crashed into us? How about we talk about how you kept this from me for two weeks? And even if I did know, why does it matter to me if he is out? I have no idea who he is. Yelling at him if I see him on the street isn't going to bring back Dean."

My parents look at each other while Kristy and Daniel stare at their food. No one moves to keep eating.

Dad turns to me. "We wanted to tell you earlier, but we weren't sure how to break the news to you. We weren't sure if you would be comfortable talking about any of it. Dean's mother has also tried to contact you, but says you decline her calls."

My crushes from the guilt. "I'm never comfortable talking about it, Dad. It brings back too many memories."

"Dean's parents told us his name."

"I don't want to know the guy's name. I don't want that man's name to be another thing for me to think about when I'm trying to move on with my life. It's only going to cause more heartache for me."

"Emma, sweetie, it might help you move on, get the closure you need. We thought that maybe now that it has been two years, you might want to at least know his name."

I look between my parents. "It's not like knowing the person will bring back Dean."

"Emma, this man is out there. We're just worried he could hurt someone else or you again," Dad says.

I pick up my fork and swirl the food around my plate with it. "How will me knowing stop him from doing so? I'm never going to cross paths with him again."

"But you should at least know his name in case you do," Daniel speaks up. "At least if you know, you can avoid him."

I frown at my brother. "I said I don't want to know his name. Like I said, knowing his name isn't going to bring back Dean."

"Well, maybe you would like to see a picture of him," Mum says, pulling up her phone.

"No, I don't want to see the picture!" I raise my voice.

Mum puts her phone down. "Emma, you should know the name of the man who was involved in the accident with you."

I drop the fork on my plate. Everyone jumps at the sound of the clatter, and I don't care. I stand up. "You know, thank you for inviting me to dinner, but I really don't want to discuss this anymore. I don't want to know the name of the person. I don't want to see a picture of him. It's never going to make a difference. And even if I do see him on the street, what am I supposed to do? Go up to him and demand why he got behind the wheel while intoxicated and killed my boyfriend?"

"I would," Daniel says, reaching for his drink. "I'd probably punch him as well for hurting you." He sips his drink.

Dad frowns at him. "You will not do that if you see him, Daniel."

Mum gives me a small smile. "Honey, sit back down and finish your dinner."

I shake my head. "No. I'm going to go. I will see you whenever."

I turn and head towards the door. No one cares to stop me or gets up to follow me. They let me walk out the door, just the way I want.

Chapter 6

Beck

Emma's not here. I was hoping to see her this morning after my mum dropped me off, but she'd already left for work.

Last night, I couldn't stop thinking about her. The apple pie was so good. As I ate it, I kept replaying what had happened down by the river, wondering what was bothering her so much that she didn't want to talk about. Would she ever give me a chance and allow me to listen to her?

Emma wasn't the only thing on my mind. I thought of Annie's offer with the spare room, and I knew it's something I needed to take. I needed this job. And if staying at the farm helps me, I can eventually rent a house in town, and have Mum move in where I know she will be safe.

When I get to work, I spot Annie in the chicken coop, collecting eggs.

"Hey, Annie, is your spare room still on offer?"

"Of course it is, Beck. If you enjoy working here, you can move into it. I would be happy to have another person living here on the farm and helping me out around."

I smile at her. "Well, do you mind if I move in on Saturday?"

"Sure, it's alright with me."

I thank her and start on with my chores for the day. Thankfully I didn't have a lot of belongings to move. Mum brought a few of my things over to Chandler's, mostly clothes, as everything else is back at home, and there's no way I'm daring to enter the house when my father is around.

I make my way towards the stables and start giving the horses fresh water and food before I muck out their stalls.

Darcy and Roxanne come in around nine to start their shift at the stables, which is a relief because I really don't know what I'm doing with them.

Later, as I'm taking out the wheelbarrow, I see Roxanne inside Blondie's stall, brushing her coat. I wonder if she and Darcy talk much with Emma. Maybe they could tell me something about her.

I approach her. "Hi, Roxanne."

Roxanne turns to me, her brown eyes lighting up when she smiles. "Hi, Beck."

"Do you mind if I ask you something?"

She stops grooming and walks over to the stall's door, leaning on it. Her long brown hair flowing over her shoulder that's tide up in a side ponytail. "Sure. What do you want to ask?"

"Do you and Darcy talk with Emma much?"

Roxanne gives me a weird look, as if wondering why I would be asking her that. "No. Emma keeps clear of us."

"She keeps clear of you?"

Roxanne nods. "Yeah, she kind of keeps to herself. She's mostly inside the guest house or with Annie. Sometimes she comes in here to be with Blondie and takes her out for a ride."

If Emma usually stays clear of Roxanne and Darcy, why did she approach me yesterday and ask me to go for a swim? Or maybe she was just being nice because I'm new.

"She's pretty much a loner," Roxanne goes on. "Darcy and I asked her to hang out with us once, but she wasn't interested."

"I see. She doesn't like to socialise with anyone?"

Roxanne shrugs. "Not really. She doesn't seem to like people much. Why do you want to know about her?"

"I'm just curious. I asked her something yesterday, and she snapped at me."

She laughs. "Yeah, she has issues or something. She never seems happy."

"Who never seems happy?" Darcy joins us, her brown ponytail moving side to side as she walked.

"Emma."

"Oh yeah. Emma. We've asked her to come out with us a few times, but she never seemed interested. We even offered to set her up with someone. She stopped talking to us after that." Darcy rolls her hazel eyes. "I don't know what her problem is."

"Maybe she has a boyfriend already?" I guess.

Roxanne scoffs. "Emma has a boyfriend? Yeah, no one comes around here except for her brother, who I think is very hot. Honestly, Beck, it's probably best you stay clear of her as well. You're better off talking to Darcy and me instead."

I look between the two ladies, not wanting to believe what they were saying about Emma. Yesterday, Emma was the one who came up to me, so she couldn't be that bad. Considering the way they speak about her, I wouldn't blame her for not talking to them.

Darcy stands closer to me, putting her hand on my bicep and squeezing it. "Do you have a girlfriend, Beck? Maybe we should go out sometime?"

I shake Darcy's hand off me. "I need to get back to work," I say before leaving the stables, not wanting to be around them any longer.

I leave the stables, not wanting to be around them any longer. I don't know Emma, but from my few moments with her yesterday, she's nothing like what Roxanne and Darcy were implying about her. Sure, she got upset with me for asking her questions about her life. Maybe she's the kind of person who keeps personal stuff to herself. Or maybe there's something going on within her life that she doesn't want me to know. I'm sure if I reveal to Roxanne and Darcy where I've been for the past two years, they wouldn't want to talk to me either. They'd possibly spread rumours about me.

As I make my way over to the chicken coop, Buckley spots me from the other side of the fence in the goat pen. He gives me an evil eye, ready to charge me if I dare to enter.

So I walk over to the goat pen and put my hand on the gate, Buckley's eye never leaving me.

"Hey, Buckley," I say to him. "Everything is good between us, isn't it, buddy? You don't really hate me, do you?"

Buckley maaahs at me.

"Maaah to you too," I answer back, opening the gate to test the waters, gripping the handle of the bucket of feed.

Immediately, Buckley is charging after me. But I don't go all the way in, and am able to quickly close the gate before I get rammed by a goat. I have never met a goat who hated someone so much. How was I supposed to change the food and water?

Behind me, I hear a burst of laughter. I turn around to see Annie walking over to me.

"Buckley really doesn't like males for some reason," she tells me.

"Yeah, Emma was telling me that yesterday."

"I'm not sure what made him like that." Annie stands beside me. "He used to be a sweet goat, and still is. He used to love my husband. Only he could go near Buckley. He would follow him everywhere. After he died a few years ago, Buckley was never the same again. Any male that entered who wasn't my husband, he would come charging after them."

"So, how can I get into the pen if he is like that?"

Annie shakes her head. "Oh, Beck, I don't really know. Just don't quit on me because of one goat. My last farmhand got so tired of getting rammed by Buckley that he left."

"You have no need to worry, Annie. I'm not going to let an angry old goat scare me away."

She smiles at me with weary eyes. "Thank you, Beck. I need all the help I can on this farm. Sometimes, I'm not sure what I'm going to do when it's my time to go. I love this place. I grew up here when my parents owned the property. My favourite thing was hanging out with the horses. I would hate to have to give them all new homes."

"Do you have any children?"

Annie smiles. "I do. I have two kids and a couple of grandkids. My kids help me every now and again, but I'm not sure if any of them will want to take over here."

"I'm sure they will, Annie."

"Well, I'd better get back inside to get dinner started. There are no riding lessons today, so Darcy and Roxanne will be leaving soon."

Good, I think. *I don't want them to be here any longer.*

"Emma should be getting home around five," Annie goes on.

I take my phone from my back pocket to have a look at the time. It's only 2:15. So it'll be another couple of hours until I hope to catch a glimpse of Emma before I leave with Mum.

Annie leaves me while I finish cleaning everything up and making sure the animals have something to eat. I leave the goats alone because Buckley isn't going to let me come in. I need a plan B to get into that pen.

I stay close by, watching for the driveway, hoping Emma will return home soon.

Chapter 7

Emma

I see Daniel talking with Annie the moment I pull in after my shift. I sigh. He's probably here because of the way I acted last night, or because Mum sent him. Either way, I wasn't in the mood for this. I get out of the car, locking it. I walk over to my brother, wondering what he could possibly want after what happened last night.

"Hey, I thought I would come by to see how you are doing," he says, slipping his hands into his pockets.

"You didn't have to come by, Daniel."

"I know. I wanted to, Emma. You left in a hurry last night."

"Sorry that I did that. I had to get away."

"I'm sorry for not saying anything to you. Mum and Dad are so sorry too."

I raise an eyebrow, crossing my arms across my chest. "Are you truly sorry? That jerk who killed Dean was out of jail for two weeks, and no one cared to tell me he was out. I get that you are worried about how I might react, but I still have the right to know, even if I may never bump into him."

"Maybe you're right, Emma. I'm sorry we never said anything to you straight away. It was hard for us to figure out how we were going to tell you because you never want to talk about the accident. You shut everyone out. I bumped into Katie the other day. She

49

asked how you are because she hardly talks to you anymore. Your own friends and family are trying to be there for you, but you keep pushing us away because all you care about is Dean. And maybe you would have known about the man being released if you just answered the phone when Dean's mother tried to call. She has been trying to reach you for weeks. Why wouldn't you answer your phone? Like I get it you don't want to talk about the accident, but for crying out loud, Emma, stop blocking out everyone like we don't exist."

I narrow my eyes at my brother. How dare he comes here, telling me what I should be doing? Is that the only reason why he came here? Put me down for not talking to anyone? Maybe I have been pushing everyone I know away since Dean died. I have never been the kind of person to do that, not until the accident. Everyone tells me to move on, but I can't let go of Dean.

"If you're here to tell me what I should be doing, then you should leave, Daniel," I snap at him.

My brother looks away from me for a second before turning back. "I'm not telling you what you should be doing. I know how deeply affected you have been with Dean's death. But it doesn't give you the right to push everyone away. I understand you might need space, and that's okay. Just don't push people away when they are trying to help you. It's been two years, Emma. You can't keep holding onto Dean forever. You need to move on and look at everyone that you have right in front of you. I can't be here when you keep pushing me away. Sometimes, I'm surprised you even talk to me. I mean, you wouldn't even answer the damn phone yesterday when Mum tried to call you once you ran out. You could have returned the call to let Mum know you were okay, but you didn't. You treat her like she doesn't even matter to you anymore. You treat everyone like that because the only person who matters to you is Dean."

Every word my brother says is a punch to my gut. Is all of that really true?

"I'm sorry for the way I've been acting. I really am. I don't know how to move on from Dean's death, okay? I have tried to, but I can't."

"You can, Emma. Let someone in, and they can help you to move on. I'm right here. If you want to talk, let's talk. If not me, Kristy will listen. Mum and Dad will listen. Even your friends. If you don't want to talk to any of us, that's fine. Talk with a counsellor or someone you feel you can trust. We can help you get through whatever you're feeling. You just need to let us in."

I nod, inhaling a deep breath. Tears prickle at my eyelids, and I'm trying so hard to blink them back so they don't fall. "What if I can't move on? What if ... what if I forget Dean when I do?"

Daniel steps closer to me. "You aren't going to forget Dean. He's going to be in your heart forever, okay? He loves you, and I don't think he would want you to push everyone away who you can turn to for help. He doesn't want you to mourn him forever. He wants you to move on and be happy."

I bite my lip, nodding. It was getting harder to stop the tears now. "I know."

"Promise me you'll let someone in? It doesn't matter who it is. Just let them in, Emma."

It's not a promise I'm sure I could keep, and I'm sure I'll break it as soon as someone tries to get me to open up about Dean.

Shutting everyone out is my way of not wanting to think about the accident. But perhaps I need to talk about it?

"Okay," I say.

Daniel pulls me into a hug. "I have to get going and meet Kristy. I'll talk to you soon. And do let Mum know that you're okay." He pulls away. "You take care, sis."

I force myself to give my brother a smile. "See you, Daniel."

I watch my brother get into his car and drive off down the driveway.

I stand there for a moment, staring up at the sky, watching the clouds above me. They predict rain later this evening, possibly a thunderstorm, but the white clouds and patches of blue sky right now don't show there will be any rain.

Wiping my eyes, I turn to head inside the guest house to change out of my work clothes. I want to ride Blondie. I've promised her a ride enough times, and it's time I keep my promise.

"Is everything alright?"

I turn to see Beck walking over to me with a face filled with concern.

I smile back at him. "Everything's okay."

"Are you sure? That guy wasn't bothering you?"

"No. That's my brother. He was just coming to check up on me."

He nods. "Alright. I just want to make sure he wasn't hassling you. I thought maybe he was your boyfriend."

My heart aches at the mention of the word. Why does it ache so much at the mention of the word?

I shake my head. "No. He is my older brother. I don't..." I bite my lip because now the tears are threatening to fall again. "I don't have a boyfriend."

As soon as I say it, my heart crumbles into a million pieces. It has taken me so long to admit that I didn't have one. At times, I still wanted to believe that Dean was still here. But he isn't here, and I remind myself that I can't call him my boyfriend anymore.

Beck steps closer to me. "You don't look okay, Emma. Are you sure everything's alright?"

I think about what my brother had just said about me opening up to someone. Anyone. Occasionally, when there's something on my mind, I might talk with Annie. I could talk with Beck. He seems like he could be the kind of person who would listen. But he's also a stranger I only just met. I don't know anything about him, nor do I know him well enough to tell him how I'm feeling. Maybe someday, but not today.

I tuck a strand of my hair that escaped my ponytail behind my ear. "I'm fine. Don't worry about me."

"I'm here if you want to talk. But if you don't, I understand."

I give him a warm smile. He reminded me of Dean's caring nature. "I'll keep that in mind."

"Great, well..." He stands awkwardly in the silence, scratching at the back of his head. "I should get back to work then."

Beck starts to turn towards the barn.

But as he does, I call out to Beck before I can stop myself.

He turns around to face me, and when he does, my stomach does a flip. "Yes?"

"I'm going to take Blondie for a walk. I promised I would take her today. If you aren't too busy, would you like to join me?"

His eyes widen at my invitation. Frankly, I'm surprised with myself for even asking.

"I would love to, but I don't know how to ride a horse," he says, and my stomach unclenches just a little.

"That's okay. I'll show you how."

"Okay. I'm about done anyway. I'm just going to let Annie know that I'm taking a break."

I nod. "Yeah, that's fine. I'm going to get changed."

After I finish changing into a simple pair of jeans and a T-shirt, I meet Beck near the stables. He's there already, standing right near Blondie's stall.

"Annie said I can go along with you," he says.

I smile. "That's great."

"So, where do you usually ride?"

"I usually just ride her to the river. Stay there for a bit to let her feed before taking her back to the stables."

"Cool. So, which horse am I riding?"

I lead him over to a stall two down from Blondie, where Raven is, a beautiful black stallion. I see Darcy and Roxanne use him for beginner riders.

"You can ride Raven," I tell him. "He is a really sweet horse. He is very gentle with beginner riders."

"That's good to know."

Once the horses are ready, we walk them out of their stalls. I demonstrate how to climb on, and Beck follows my actions. He has no trouble climbing up onto the horse, almost like he has done this a million times.

I smile. "Good. Now let's get going."

Chapter 8

Beck

Emma is right, Raven is a sweet and gentle horse. It's like he senses that I'm only a beginner and takes his steps slowly, matching his steps with Blondie's. According to Emma, I look stiff as I hold the reins. When she tells me to relax, I listen to her, admiring how natural she was on a horse.

"How did you learn how to ride?" I ask.

"I took a few lessons from Darcy and Roxanne," Emma explains. "Then I stopped and just learned to ride by myself, taking Blondie out for walks when I felt like I needed to get away from the farm for a bit, or I just wanted to be alone."

I think of the conversation I had with those ladies earlier today.

"Can I ask you something? What happened between you, Darcy and Roxanne? I was asking them about you, and all they did was speak badly and told me to stay away."

Emma glances my way, looking at me like she's trying to figure me out. "You were asking about me?"

I blush. "Yeah, I was just curious about you, especially with what happened yesterday. I thought I would ask them what they knew about you."

I try to read her expression, but I can't. She turns away and looks ahead.

"Ignore everything they say about me," she says. "Nothing they can say is nice."

"What happened between you guys?"

"We are just different people. They prefer to party, I don't. They want me to hook up with someone because they think I should have a boyfriend, but I don't want to hook up with some random guy. And right now, I don't exactly want to be with someone."

My heart crumbles at her words, though I'm not entirely sure why.

"Fair enough," I answer.

"So, it's your second day. How are you finding the job?"

I nod. "It's good. Just trying to figure out how to get into the goat pen."

Emma laughs. The sound of it makes my stomach do somersaults. "Buckley will get used to you eventually. Maybe try to bribe him with food. It might work."

"I'll give it a try tomorrow."

"Did you have a chance to try my apple pie?"

I almost moan at the mention of it.

"I did," I answer. "I shared it with my friend and his girlfriend. It was so good, Emma. It was honestly the best apple pie I have ever had."

Emma blushes. "You're just saying that to make me happy."

"No, I'm not. It was really good. Where did you learn how to bake?"

"I used to bake desserts with my grandmother growing up until she passed away a few years ago. I mostly baked cupcakes with my grandmother, but I have made a few pastries with her as well. Then when ... after this accident I was in, I baked to keep my mind off things."

"Do you think you can bake me another one?"

I smile. "Of course I can." She nods towards me. "You're doing very well for your first time on a horse."

"Yeah? Maybe I have a good teacher."

Emma laughs. "I'm not that great of a teacher."

"Well, I haven't fallen off yet, so you must be."

"Don't thank me. Thank Raven. I told you he is great with beginners."

I pat Raven's mane. "Thank you, Raven. You're a great horse."

Raven neighs happily in response.

We soon reach the river and get off the horses, allowing them to eat some grass. Emma and I sit down by the river.

"You're not swimming today?" I ask.

Emma shakes her head. "I don't feel like it today. Besides, it isn't so hot."

"Yeah, the weather's good today."

"So, Beck. You know a little about me. Tell me something about you."

What could I tell her about me? I'm not sure what to tell her without having her think I was some kind of murderer. Would she even want to hang out with me if she knew about my criminal record? Would she judge me? Emma seems like a great person, and I don't want to ruin her first impression of me.

Not just me having a record, but the kind of person I have grown up to be. With all of the physical and verbal abuse I have been through, I have never believed in myself. And with my criminal record and the incident following me, Emma wouldn't be interested.

"You don't want to know about me," I tell her.

She tilts her head. "Why not? You seem like a great guy. Tell me anything about yourself. It can be anything. What's your favourite sport?"

"Football."

Emma wrinkles her nose. "I can't stand football."

"Why not? It's a great sport."

"It's a stupid sport if you ask me. I mean, all you do is tackle the other person and I don't understand that."

I laugh. "Then you need to understand it. Maybe I should invite you to a football game someday."

"Please do not ever do that. Anyway, what else should I know about you?"

I bite my lip, thinking what can I tell her about me? All I can think about is what she will think if she knew the real me.

I shake my head. "There isn't anything else you need to know."

Emma watches me like she's trying to figure me out again, the same way I was trying to figure out what could be bothering her. Can she see right through me?

"Tell you what," I go on. "I'll tell you my secret if you tell me yours."

She turns away, looking out at the river. "I told you, I don't want to talk about it."

I nod. "I totally understand. When we're ready, we both can reveal secrets about ourselves that we don't like to discuss with others."

"So you aren't going to tell me anything about yourself? Like where you're from and what you like to do?"

"Telling you all of that requires me to tell you about the secret, and I don't want you to judge me just yet."

Emma glances over her shoulder at the horses before turning back to me. "Okay. Deal. I'll tell you when I get to know you a bit more and when I can trust you."

I hold out my hand for her to shake. "Deal."

She looks at my hand and then shakes it before standing up.

"We should get going and bring the horses back before it gets dark. Are you staying for dinner with Annie and me?"

I get to my feet. "No, not tonight. My mum is picking me up soon. But I'm moving into the guest room on Saturday, so probably then."

"Okay, fair enough." She walks over to Blondie, stroking the horse's mane. "Maybe I will make another pie for dessert on Saturday."

I smile at her. "That sounds good. Can't wait."

Emma mounts up onto Blondie. "Come on, mount up."

I mount up onto Raven with the way she showed me.

Once we get back to the stables and place the horses in their stalls, I really don't want to leave. I want to stay here with Emma, get to know her more, even if she won't tell me about herself. Was it something to do with the boyfriend she said she didn't have? I wonder, but for now, I just needed to wait for her to get to know me more so she would tell me. Then I will have to work up the courage to tell her about my crappy life that I prefer doesn't exist.

"How's the job going?" Chandler asks later that evening when we were sitting out on the balcony.

He was drinking a bottle of beer, and it was so hard for me to not go into the fridge and grab myself one

"The job is great," I answer. "I mean, it's not like the perfect job, but at least I was accepted, despite my record."

Chandler takes a sip of his beer. "I don't know how you could work there and come home smelling like horse manure every day."

I chuckle. "Yeah, well, that's the downside of the job."

"Is there an upside to it?"

Emma crosses my mind, her beautiful smile lighting up her blue eyes. The thought of her sends butterflies dancing around my stomach.

"You know the girl who baked the apple pie the other day?"

Chandler nods. "Yeah, the one you said who lives on the farm with your boss?"

"Yeah, she's ... she's beautiful, Chandler. She's nice, even though she seems to be the kind of person to keep to herself. I've been hanging out with her for the last two days. We kind of got off on the wrong foot yesterday, but today was better. I guess we just need to get to know each other a bit more. She seems like this incredible woman, and I want to get to know her more."

Chandler smiles. "After everything that has happened to you, Beck, I'm really happy for you. You got this job; you're moving out, and perhaps you might get the girl."

"I don't know about moving out. I mean, I'm not exactly getting my own place."

"No, but you're renting out your boss's room. Maybe soon you will be able to get your own place."

I nod. Chandler's right. "I plan to do that. I plan to get my own place and move my mother in with me, get her far away from that bastard." We sit there in silence for a moment. "Chandler, tell me, how bad did it get with my Mum while I was in jail? I know something has happened recently, but Mum tells me not to worry."

Chandler takes a sip of his drink, finishing it up before placing the empty bottle on the table between us. "Terrible, Beck. I check in on her every now and again. She also spent some nights here when things got bad at your place. Lisa and I took care of her, making sure she had everything she needed."

Knowing what my dad was doing to my mum while I was in jail made me wish I hadn't gone. And with me not being able to go back home or anywhere near my dad, I felt helpless sitting in Chandler's apartment, unable to help my mother.

"I should have done a lot more in my teens to get my mother and me out from there," I say. "For twenty-three years, Chandler, twenty-three years my mother has put up with this abuse from my father. She could have left or asked for help, but she didn't."

"Maybe she didn't think she had the support she needed to flee," Chandler points out. "Being in a domestic violence relationship, let alone a marriage, isn't difficult to get out of. I mean, yeah, you have the opportunity to leave. But many fear because they may not have somewhere to go or they have no support for what they are going through. Plus, your father probably threatened her a lot, so the threats stopped her from leaving."

True. Mum didn't have family support. She hasn't spoken to my grandparents since they kicked her out of the house for getting pregnant with me at sixteen. I was Mum's only support. And it wasn't like Mum could take me and live somewhere else because she didn't have money. Any earnings she made with her job, Dad took.

"Thank you, Chandler, and to Lisa also, for helping my mum while I was gone."

Chandler smiles. "It's no problem, Beck. I just want you and your mum to have a good life. You both need it. So work hard on this job so you can get your own place and have your mother move in with you. You both need this. If your mother wasn't able to escape when you were younger, you can help her escape now. It will just mean I won't be able to invite you over to my place in case your dad finds you here."

"I know, but you and Lisa are welcome to come visit whenever you want, when I save for my own place."

"I'm sure she'll appreciate the help she gets from you and everything that you're doing to get yourself help so you can be a better person. More than what your father will ever be."

Chandler is right. I can picture my new life once I earn enough money to move into my own place, possibly somewhere in Maisy Grove or near the farm. Mum will live with me. And maybe I will be able to make Emma my girl too.

That's if she is interested in me.

Chapter 9

Emma

I lie there in the darkness of my bed, thinking of what Beck could be hiding about his past. I think about what my brother had said to me the other day, and I wonder if Beck could be the kind of person I would eventually let in.

Each day after work this week, Beck and I have hung out. There's this easy connection between us that I'm sure he can feel too. Something about him that makes me feel safe, that for those small moments, I can forget everything that has happened in my life. But the thought of seeing someone new, I don't know…

It's Saturday, and I get up to help Annie load her truck for the farmer's market.

"Thank you, dear," she says once we finish loading.

I smile at her and walk around to the passenger side door to hop in.

"Actually, Emma, I was wondering if you could stay behind today."

I stare at her, puzzled. "What? Why? I always help you at the farmer's market."

Annie gives me a warm smile. "I know, Emma, and I appreciate all of the help you do for me. But today, I'm going to head to the market on my own. I want you to stay at the farm today. Beck will be coming sometime this morning with his friend to move his belongings into his room. I just need someone to be here while I'm out. Do you think you can help Beck?"

I stare at Annie, wondering what she's up to, my stomach filling with butterflies. Why didn't she discuss this with me yesterday? And why did she want me to help Beck? I didn't help the last employee that moved into Annie's spare room. Instead, she stayed here while I worked at the market.

"Are you sure, Annie?" I ask. "What about you? Are you going to be alright at the market?"

Annie waves it off like it's no big deal. "Oh, honey, don't worry about me. I'll be fine. All you need to do is help Beck get settled in. He seems to be quite comfortable around you, so I'm sure he will appreciate you helping him."

I close the door. "Okay, if you say so."

Annie smiles. "Thank you, Emma. I'm not sure what time he's coming, but he said it will be sometime this morning."

Annie walks around to the driver's side. "Let me know if you need anything."

She hops into the truck and makes her way down the driveway. I watch her until I can't see the trail lights anymore.

I pull out my phone. It's almost five o'clock. In the meantime, I decide to head back inside the house and wait until Beck arrives, thinking of baking a pie as a welcoming present. Yes, that's what I'll do.

I start working on the pastry, deciding on filling it with blueberries this time.

While the pie bakes, I head outside when I hear Rocky the rooster waking everyone up. I grab a basket, set a timer on my phone to remind me when to take my pie out of the oven and head out to collect the eggs. By the time I finish up, I check the timer on my phone. I still have half an hour to go before I head back to the oven.

I take the basket back to my house, checking on the pie while I'm there. The pastry smells delicious, its aroma filling up the whole house. I decide to stay inside now, knowing the pie is almost done. I settle on the couch to read a book while I wait. Soon enough, the timer soon goes off, and I take it out of the oven, setting it down on the cooling rack.

I then head outside to make a start on the goats, filling their water and food.

When I'm just about done with them, a car pulls up outside Annie's house. In the passenger seat, I can see Beck getting out of the car with another guy at the wheel.

"Ugh, this place stinks," the guy says. "Glad I'm not working here." He turns to Beck. "Are you sure you want to move here?"

"I'm sure." Beck walks to the back of the car.

I head over to the guys.

"Hey, Beck."

He turns around to see me coming towards them. He smiles. "Hi, Emma." He waves me over. "Come here. I would like you to meet my good friend."

He gestures towards his friend. "Emma, I want you to meet Chandler." He gestures to me next. "Chandler, meet Emma. She lives on the farm with Annie."

Chandler smiles at me, extending his hand, and I shake it. "It's nice to meet you, Emma."

I return the smile. "It's nice to meet you too." I turn to Beck. "Would you like me to help you bring your things inside?"

"Sure," Beck says. "Where's Annie?"

"Annie is at the farmer's market," I explain. "She should be back around one o'clock. She's asked me to stay to help you."

I unlock the front door first, placing a door stop in front to keep it open. I then help the guys carry a few boxes inside to the spare room. Beck doesn't have many things, just a few boxes with clothes in them. It was like he lived a simple life. I catch a glimpse of photograph sticking out on top of the box I was carrying, showing a young Beck on his bike. Outdoorsy is the first thing that comes to mind of him, remembering how he liked football. A small smile spreads across my lips as I think of Dean, how he was such an outgoing and outdoorsy person.

I have only been to the spare room once, helping the last farmhand with moving his stuff out of the room. There's a double bed in the corner, a wardrobe to the other side, along with a couch and a television. Annie had offered me the room once, but I declined. I liked the privacy I get in the guest house.

"This is where you'll be staying," I say.

Chandler and Beck put their boxes down beside the door, and I place my box beside them.

"What do you think, Beck?" Chandler asks. "If you don't like it here, you are welcome to come back to my place."

Beck glances around the room. "It seems nice and cosy in here. I'll see how everything goes, and if I don't like it here, I'll let you know."

I give him a smile. "Is there anything else you want from the car?"

Beck shakes his head. "No, I'm right with everything. Thank you, Emma."

"I'll let you guys be alone. If you need me, I'll be outside."

I leave the guys alone and head out to the stables to check on the horses. I see Darcy's and Roxanne's cars and groan. I really wasn't in the mood to see those two, even though I know they have riding lessons this morning. Kids will soon start arriving.

I enter the stables, and to my relief, Darcy and Roxanne are nowhere to be seen, so I head straight over to Blondie. She's eating some hay in her stall, and when she sees me, she trots over, placing her head over the door.

"Hey, girl," I pat her mane. "How are you today?"

Blondie neighs.

"That's good to hear."

"There you are, Emma," Darcy's voice rings out of nowhere. "Where have you been this morning?"

"With Beck?" Roxanne adds.

I turn to see the two of them walking over to me. I ignore them both and turn back to Blondie, running a hand on her snout.

"We saw you with Beck," Roxanne goes on when I don't answer her. "You were helping him move his things into the house."

"Is there something going on between you two?" Darcy wants to know. "You two have been hanging around each other every afternoon this week."

I roll my eyes, sighing and turn to them. "It's none of your business what Beck and I have been doing. And no, nothing is going on between us. We're just friends."

"Friends, huh? Is that what you're calling it? Funny, because you don't act friendly with us."

"Yes, and you wonder why I don't."

Darcy narrows her eyes at me. "What do you mean by that?"

"Look, I don't like you because of the kind of people you are. I mean, you'd rather party or hook up with guys. I'm not interested in that kind of stuff."

Roxanne laughs. "Wow, Emma. You really need to get laid. Maybe you should talk to Beck about it. I'm sure he'll be happy to help you out."

I frown at them. Who do they think they are to talk to me like that? "Don't speak that way to me again. I'm not some slut like you both are. I'm not interested in sleeping around with random men. I'd rather be in a relationship with someone I want to be with for the rest of my life. Not someone I can have fun with for a little while."

"Oh, honey," Darcy says with a smirk, "what century are you living in? Nowadays, people would rather have benefits than settle down in a relationship."

I clench my fist. "Well, I'm not some people. I don't want benefits. I want a relationship. And I definitely don't need the two of you trying to set me up with anyone."

Without another word, I walk past them. I hear Darcy mumble something softly that I'm sure isn't nice, and I don't care what she has to say. She can say whatever she wants about me, but I'm never going to be like her.

And yeah, Beck seems like a nice guy, but I don't know if I want to be in another relationship with someone else. I'm still in love with Dean. Maybe I should be moving on instead of living in the past, but not like this.

Chapter 10

Beck

Chandler hangs out in my room for a bit before leaving to let me settle in. I unpack my belongings before going out to find Emma.

I find her leaning on the fence of the goats' pen.

"Hey, Emma," I call out.

She looks up at me and then quickly turns, wiping her eyes. "Yeah?"

I look closer, my stomach dropping. "Emma, what's wrong? Are you crying?"

Emma sniffs, not looking at me. "No."

I reach her and rest a hand on her arm. "You are. What happened?"

She turns to look at me, her eyes red and puffy. My heart crumbles. "Nothing. Don't worry about it."

"It's not nothing. Tell me what's the matter?"

Emma looks past my shoulder before looking back at me. "I'm just sick and tired of Darcy and Roxanne always thinking I should be hooking up with someone. They think if I get laid, I'll be happy." She shakes her head. "That will never make me happy."

"Is there a reason why it wouldn't?"

She looks away, watching the goats. "Because I don't want that. I want to be with the person who made me happy, who I wanted to spend the rest of my life with. I can never do that."

"Why can't you be with them?"

She doesn't say anything at first. "Because my boyfriend is dead."

My heart aches at her words.

"I'm sorry to hear that, Emma. I really am."

She gives me a small, sad smile. "Thanks."

I look over my shoulder and see Roxanne and Darcy by the stables, watching us, whispering about something. Frowning, I wonder who those girls think they are, but they have no right to do what they do. I understand clearly now why Emma wants nothing to do with them.

I began making my way over to them.

"Where are you going, Beck?" Emma calls out to me.

I didn't listen to her as I made my way over to the girls. Emma catches up to me and grabs my arm.

"No," she says. "You will make it worst."

I turn to her. "How can I make it worst?" I gesture towards the girls. "They are bullying you, Emma. Don't let them bully you."

"I know, but just don't do anything. They might get you into trouble."

"They won't if I tell Annie what they have been doing to you."

"Don't approach them, please? Just leave it alone."

She drops my arm and turns back to the goat pen.

I follow her. "Can I ask you something? I mean, don't take this the wrong way, but have you tried to do anything that might help you move on from your boyfriend?"

Emma shakes her head. "No. Can we drop this? Forget I even said anything."

We reach the goat pen. Emma leans up against the fence, watching the goats.

I stand next to her. "How do you feel if I help you with moving on?"

Emma turns to face me. "And how are you going to help me?"

"What if you met someone, and it helps you? I mean, maybe Darcy and Roxanne setting you up with someone won't be so bad. It could help you move on."

She thinks about it for a moment. "No. I'm not exactly looking to be with someone right now. And I most definitely don't want to be set up with someone by them."

"What kind of guy would you like to be with?"

Emma smiles. "Someone who is caring and honest. Someone I know I can always count on."

I smile at her. "Okay, well maybe you can meet someone like that, but you won't until you try."

Her smile fades and she shakes her head. "No. I don't believe I will ever be able to move on from Dean. He's someone I love deeply, and no one could ever replace him."

I look over at Darcy and Roxanne, who laugh at something. An idea hits me, but not sure how Emma will take it.

"Don't take it the wrong way, but I think I know a way to get Darcy and Roxanne off your back."

She tilts her head. "How?"

"What if we pretend we are together? Maybe they will leave you alone about setting you up with someone?"

Emma takes a step back from me. "No. That will never work."

"How would you know it wouldn't?"

"It just wouldn't. They will know it's an act."

"Just trust me, Emma." I step forward and reach out to take her hand in mine.

She shakes my hand off me and takes another step backwards. "I don't know you well, Beck. How can I trust you?"

She has a point. How can she trust me? Especially when I'm a mess up person, trying to make my life better.

"You're right," I say. "You don't know me well enough to trust me. But you can if you were to open up and allow me in. And right now, I want to help you with getting Darcy and Roxanne off your back."

"Even if you could, how could us being together help get them off my back? I mean, they will want to know every single detail of our relationship."

"They don't need to know anything."

Emma looks past my shoulder, then back at me.

"Are they still watching?" I ask.

Emma nods. "They are. Beck, this idea of yours isn't going to work."

"You don't know it won't."

"Well, show me. If you want me to trust you with this, show me how us pretending to be together will get them off my back."

I step forward and take her hands into mine. She observes me, and her breath hitches from my touch.

"Would you feel comfortable if I was to kiss you right now?"

Her eyes widen. "What?" She shakes her head and drops my hands. "I just told you that my boyfriend died, and you want to kiss me? For what? To pretend we are together in front of Darcy and Roxanne?"

The way she says it makes me feel so dumb. Of course she won't feel comfortable. She doesn't even know me.

"In order to make this believable, a kiss will convince them we are together."

Emma shakes her head. "I don't want to kiss you."

"But this could work, Emma. Please, just trust me on this. Look, I'm sorry. It's stupid of me to ask you this. It's all I could think of to help you. Maybe there's a better way to approach this, but this is the first thing that popped into my mind."

"What if we did kiss, and they still bully me?"

"Then it's up to you to tell Annie how they treat you. I want to help you get those girls off your back, and I think this is one way they will leave you alone."

Emma looks past my shoulder, then back at me. I see the worry in her eyes, like she was scared of something. "Are you sure this will work?"

"I think it will."

"If I say yes, will the kiss mean anything?"

"Do you want it to mean something?"

"No. I don't. It's just that I haven't kissed anyone in a very long time."

"That's okay. I will take it slowly."

Emma bites her lip, then nods. "Okay. You can kiss me."

My heart flutters in my chest when she says it. I step closer to her, putting a hand on her waist and with the other hand, I tuck a strand of her hair behind her ear. I watch her carefully, seeing the nervousness in her gorgeous blue eyes. I stroke her cheek.

"Are you sure I can kiss you?" I double-check.

She nods. "If you are sure this plan will work, then I will let you kiss me this once. But nothing can come between us. I'm not looking for a relationship."

I nod. "Got it."

I lean forward, and as I do, I see Emma holding her breath. My hand cups her jaw as my lips brush hers. I flutter my eyes closed, kissing her slowly and softly like I had promised her I would. I give her a short kiss before pulling away.

Emma's eyes are closed when I pull away. She keeps them closed for a few short seconds before opening her eyes again. We stare at each other. Whether or not the kiss was a good thing, there's some kind of connection between us. I could feel it, and all I want to do is kiss her again. I'm sure she did too, but we don't make the move to do it again.

Emma turns away first, looking past my shoulders. "They're gone now. Are you sure about what you said? That this will give them something to gossip about? To get them off my back?"

I nod. "I'm sure. And if they give you a hard time, Emma, let me deal with them. They have no right to treat you the way they do. Does Annie know how they treat you?"

She shakes her head. "No. She doesn't know. I never told her. I don't want to cause any trouble."

"You won't be causing trouble if they are the ones harassing you."

"Well, I hope what you did will help them to back off me a little."

"Like I said, if they don't, let me deal with it."

She opens her mouth to say something, but we hear tyres crunching on the gravel driveway. We turn to see Annie pulling in.

She parks her truck next to Emma's. We walk over to ask her how the market was.

Annie gets out of the truck and smiles at us. "It was great. And it's good to see you, Beck. Everything okay with in the move?"

"Yes, everything went well. Emma helped with everything."

"That's good to hear."

Jessie comes bounding over to Annie. Annie kneels down and scratches her behind the ears.

"Hello, girl," Annie greets her, then she looks up at Emma. "Has Jessie eaten yet?"

"Probably," Emma says. "I filled her bowl up, but I have no idea if she has eaten or not. She's been sleeping near my guest house for most of the morning and wandering around the farm."

Annie stands up. "How about you two? Have you eaten yet?"

I shake my head. "No. Not yet."

"Well, come on inside. I'll prepare lunch for you."

"Great."

"It's okay, Annie." Emma shakes her head. "I have already eaten something."

"Okay." Annie turns to me. "Come on inside when you're ready."

Annie heads inside with Jessie at her heels. I didn't see Jessie when I arrived this morning, and I wonder if she really was sleeping like Emma said.

I turn to Emma. She isn't making eye contact with me. She then turns to head to her guest house without another word. I wonder if she really did eat something earlier or if maybe she's avoiding me because of the kiss. Damn it. Why did I kiss her? It was a dick move, especially after what she had told me. We've only just met.

We don't even know each other well. Yet, all I want to do is help her and give Darcy and Roxanne something to talk about. Will it help if they think I'm really Emma's boyfriend? I don't know.

I look over my shoulder to see if they're around, but I don't see them. They're probably getting ready for their lessons. Good. I hope they don't give Emma too much of a hard time. They shouldn't.

I head inside and enter the kitchen, where Annie is making a ham and cheese sandwich for both of us. I sit down at the table, and she sets a plate down in front of me. I thank her, and she sits across from me.

"So, have you settled in yet?" Annie asks.

"I think so. I have unpacked a few of my things."

"That's good. Make yourself feel at home as much as possible."

"Thank you again, Annie, for allowing me to stay here."

Annie waves it off like it's no big deal. "No need to thank me. I'm just doing something that I thought would be easier for you."

We eat in silence for a few minutes. As I eat, all I can think about is Emma and the kiss. I wonder if Emma would let me kiss her again...

No. I shouldn't be thinking that. She said she doesn't want a relationship.

"How are you and Emma getting along?" Annie interrupts my thoughts. "I see the two of you hanging around for the past week. I'm happy you sorted everything out between you two."

"I am too. I think we're getting along well."

"Remember, if you want to be let in with any of her secrets, you just have to show her that you will listen and that she is able to trust you, and maybe she will tell you everything."

I nod, biting into my sandwich. "Emma was upset about something earlier, and she said that her boyfriend is dead."

"That's correct."

"What happened to him? How did he die?"

Annie gives me a warm smile that tells me she isn't going to spill anything. Whatever I want to know about Emma, I just have to wait and see when she opens up to me. "Like I said, that's for Emma to tell you. She'll tell you when she's ready."

I nod. There really isn't anything else for me to do. Hopefully I didn't ruin anything with her from the kiss.

Thinking of the kiss made me think of Darcy and Roxanne and how they treat Emma.

"Annie, about Emma being upset today," I tell her. "It wasn't because she was upset about her boyfriend. She was upset because Darcy and Roxanne had said something to her. Are you aware that they sometimes say nasty stuff to her?"

Annie shakes her head. "No, I wasn't aware. Emma has never mentioned it to me. How long has this been going on for?'

I shrug. "I don't know. She never said anything."

"Okay, well perhaps I'll speak to them about it. Maybe I'll also talk to Emma. Thank you, Beck, for bringing that up to me."

"It's no problem at all."

After lunch, I decide to help Annie wash up, but she only shoos me out of the kitchen.

So, I head outside to figure out what to do. Annie said I don't need to work today since it's my moving day, but I walk around the farm anyway to see how the animals are doing. I glance over at the guest house a few times, wondering if Emma is alright, but I figure she might need some space. When she's ready, she'll come to me. Maybe she needs time to process the kiss from earlier.

I walk over to the stables where all of the horses were in use this afternoon. Darcy and Roxanne have already mucked out the stalls and fed the horses, but I decide to check the stalls anyway, making sure they have enough food and water.

"What are you doing in here?"

I turn around to see Darcy, who had walked in from outside. "Just checking to see all of the stalls are fine."

She crosses her arms across her chest. "Roxanne and I have already cleaned everything."

"Okay. Just wanted to double-check to make sure everything is alright in here. I'm going to leave now."

"Hold it," Darcy says before I can leave. She frowns at me. "What is going on between you and Emma? We saw you kiss earlier."

I smirk, ready to put my plan into action. Whether they believe me, I don't care. I just want them to back off on Emma. "Didn't you know? She's my girlfriend."

Darcy laughs. "Yeah, right. You and Emma together? She has not been with anyone since Roxanne and I started working here. We've even offered to set her up with some guys, but she was never interested."

"Well, now you know why she wasn't interested. Also, both you and Roxanne can stop putting Emma down."

Darcy looks at me with a puzzled look. "What are you talking about? We don't make fun of Emma."

I scoff. She can deny all she wants, but I'm not blind nor deaf.

Without saying anything else, I walk towards the exit.

"You should be careful of her," Darcy calls out to me.

I turn around while still walking backwards. "And why should I do that?"

"She's weird. I mean, she goes off at Roxanne and me for the littlest things when we talk to her."

I arch my eyebrow at her. Did she really think she was the innocent person here?

I badly want to say something about what I actually think of her and Roxanne, but I keep my mouth shut. The last thing I need is to lose this job. I also need to get along with them both when cleaning out the stables. The last thing I want is for them to make it harder for me to do my job.

I leave, heading back to my new room, where I know I'll be until dinner. And at least while I am alone in my room, I can think about Emma.

Chapter 11

Emma

Why did you let him kiss you?
  Why did you let him kiss you?
  Why did you let him kiss you?
  Why did you let him kiss you?
  Why did you let him kiss you?

I sit on the couch, sipping a cup of tea and replaying the kiss over and over again, trying to figure out how I feel about it all. I haven't kissed anyone since kissing Dean for the last time on our formal night. I still hear the music from the night, as we dance and even shared a kiss when the teachers weren't looking. His kisses always sent a warm buzzing feeling throughout my body. Butterflies dance their way around my stomach. How is Beck feeling right now? Is he feeling anything? He said the kiss wouldn't mean anything, but I would be lying to myself if I didn't think it did. I wouldn't have butterflies.

But the kiss with Beck was different from my first kiss with Dean. Kissing Dean, I was on cloud nine, but with Beck, I didn't get that feeling. Maybe because Dean was my first kiss. With Beck, there's a spark of excitement. Like something I have been longing for a long time and wasn't aware of what I needed. While butterflies dance around my stomach, the other half of me is covered in guilt for being with someone else who's not Dean. He may have been gone for two years, and being with someone else shouldn't make me feel guilty. I'm not cheating on Dean, so why does it feel like I am?

Beck has only been here for a week, but that didn't stop me from feeling all kinds of things whenever I was around him. And this kiss only made it worse. Okay, maybe not worse, but now I don't know what I'm supposed to be feeling.

Or maybe I know what I should be feeling, but my brain is trying to protect me from being hurt again.

Could Beck be my reason for moving on from Dean? Am I ready to be in another relationship? And if I do move on, will I forget about Dean? I don't want to forget him. Yet, if I'm to put all of my attention on Beck, Dean would just slip away from me, wouldn't he?

Maybe I'm overthinking things. I mean, Annie and my brother keep telling me how I need to move on. Although, Annie is more sympathetic about it than Daniel. She tells me that when I'm ready, I will be able to move on. Maybe she understands me more than my brother. She did go through the same thing when her husband passed away.

I force myself off the couch when my tea is finished and walk over to the sink to rinse it out. Placing the cup on the drying rack, I glance outside the window, where I see Beck playing fetch with Jessie. At the sight of him, my lips curl into a smile. Maybe this is how it feels when a new person walks into your life unexpectedly and changes everything.

This is crazy. I know Dean would want me to move on and be happy. But still, how do you let go of someone you loved so much and carry on like it doesn't matter that they're gone? Does life just go on?

I stay in the guesthouse for the rest of the day until I decide to bring the pie over to Annie's. She's in the kitchen when I walk in, the smell of roast beef and vegetables fill the room.

"Mmm, smells good," I say.

Annie turns to me as she is tossing a salad. "Thank you, dear."

"I made a pie for dessert."

"That's great, Emma. It isn't because of our new guest, is it?"

I nod, placing the pie down on the counter, keeping it covered so flies can't get to it. "I thought it would be nice to bake something to celebrate him moving in."

"I'm sure Beck will appreciate that thought."

"I hope so."

I begin setting the table.

"You and Beck are getting along well," Annie says.

With my back turned to Annie, a smile crosses my face at the mention of his name. "Yeah, I guess so."

"I haven't seen you get along really well with someone. You usually keep your distance from anyone who works here, like the last farmhand. You didn't get along really well with Mike. Or even with Roxanne or Darcy."

My smile fades. "Mike never spoke to me much either. And Darcy and Roxanne, they aren't exactly the kind of people I like hanging out with."

"Yes, Beck was telling me what they've been doing to you, Emma." I turn to her. "What did they upset you about?"

I shrug, placing the cutlery on the placemats. "They just want to set me up with someone. I'm not looking for a relationship."

"And the things they say upset you because of Dean?"

"It makes me think about him. I mean, they just want me to hook up with someone, get laid but not be in a relationship. I don't exactly want to have benefits with someone. If anything, I want to be in an actual relationship. But I don't know if that's something I will ever do again."

"Never say never, Emma. When the right guy comes along, you will know. Dean will always be in your heart, but he wouldn't want you to be unhappy. He'd want you to find someone who can make you happy like he did. And if you want, I can chat with Roxanne and Darcy about being careful of what they say around you. They don't know about Dean, sweetie. Maybe they want to try to help you get out there and meet someone."

"It's okay. You don't need to say anything."

I walk over to the top cabinet and grab three tall glasses.

I place them down on the counter and turn to face Annie, where she's adding the creamy dressing to the salad. "Annie, how long did it take for you to move on from losing your husband?"

Annie puts the bottle of dressing down and turns to me. "It took me a long time. Pierce was my high school sweetheart. We'd been together since we were sixteen. Married for forty-one years. Loving someone for that long and then suddenly losing them, it's not easy to move on from, Emma. It really isn't. But it's something we all have to do eventually. We can't keep holding onto the past. We have to look at what we have in the present."

"How did Pierce die?"

"Heart attack. He was only sixty-one."

"Do you think you will ever fall in love again?"

"I don't know. I'm only seventy, but who knows if I'll ever remarry and settle down with another person. For now, I'm just enjoying living here on the farm with my animals. Christmas is next month, and my kids will be coming to visit with my grandkids, and honestly, I'm just happy to have them. Even if I don't ever meet another person, I'm happy with my kids and grandchildren."

I smile. "That's sweet. Annie. How do you know when you're ready to move on?"

Annie grabs tongs and places them in the salad bowl. "Only you know when you're ready to move on. Sometimes we may be scared to take new steps in a new direction, but you will know when it's time to move on." She looks in my direction with a smile. "This hasn't got anything to do with Beck, does it?"

I blush at the thought that Annie knew what I was thinking. "No. Why would it be?"

Annie gives me a look to say, 'You can't fool me'. "Emma, I was in love once before. I know you're still grieving Dean, but I've seen the way you and Beck have been getting along this past week. Maybe you don't realise it yourself yet, but I'm sure you have feelings for him."

I look around, making sure Beck isn't around.

"It's okay. Beck's outside," Annie says like she knew exactly what I was looking for. "There's a prediction for a storm later tonight, and I asked him to make sure all of the animals are safe in their pens and the stables."

I turn back to her, leaning up against a chair. "He's kind of cute, but I don't know how I feel about him. When I'm around him, there are these butterflies that I haven't felt since dating Dean. And this afternoon, just right before you came home, we kissed." I blushed. "It was a soft, gentle kiss that he said wouldn't mean anything. I think, in a way, he kissed me to make me feel better, even though he said he wanted to give Darcy and Roxanne something to gossip about. I mean, we've been talking all week, and I don't know if they know something is going on between us, but Beck and I don't realise it yet. He said he will help me to move on. In what way, I don't know. Now that we've kissed, I don't know what I should be feeling. Part of me feels guilty for liking someone other than Dean."

Annie smiles as she walks over to me and then pulls me into a hug. "Oh, Emma, there is nothing to feel guilty about." She pulls away from me and rests her hands on my arms. "It's part of human nature to fall in love. Dean, I'm sure, would be happy if you were to move on and fall in love with someone else. He wouldn't want you to spend the rest of your life mourning him when you can get out there and do everything you've ever wanted. The things you wanted to do with him, he would want you to do with the new person you fall in love with." She gives me an assuring smile. "It's okay to like someone else who isn't Dean."

As I process her words, I wonder if this is part of moving on. Am I able to fall in love with someone and move on? The thought seems scary.

"What if I move on, fall in love with someone else, and forget about Dean?" I look away. In a soft voice, I say, "I don't want to forget Dean."

Annie rests a hand on my cheek and then turns my face towards her. "Emma, listen to me. You will never forget about Dean. You can move on and date as many guys as you want until you find the one, but that doesn't mean you have to forget about him. Dean will always be in your heart and in the back of your mind. There are going to be things that might trigger your memory of him, but over time, I promise you moving on will get easier. You can't forget your first love. Also, I want you to be careful around Beck. I don't want you getting hurt."

I open my mouth to say something else, but before I can, the front door opens. Annie and I move away from each other just as Jessie comes running around the corner, greeting us both. Beck follows straight after, and as he walks into the kitchen, my heart skips a beat.

"Dinner smells good," he says. "All of the animals are safe in their pens and the stables in case that storm does come."

Annie smiles. "Thank you so much, Beck. Now, why don't you sit down, and I will start serving the food."

"Sounds great." He sits down at the table. "I'm starving."

Annie takes the salad bowl to the table. I walk over to the fridge and grab a clear jug of homemade lemonade Annie had made and place the jug on the table while Annie plates up the food.

"Would you like some lemonade, Beck?" I ask. "Annie made it."

"Homemade lemonade? I won't say no to that."

He holds up his glass, and I pour him a drink. I pour Annie and myself some as well before I settle into the seat across from him.

Beck takes a sip of the drink. "Mmm. Annie, this lemonade is great."

Annie walks over to the table with two plates. "Thank you."

She places one down in front of me and the other one in front of Beck before joining us.

Beck picks up his knife and fork and starts cutting into the roast beef. "Yum, roast beef. I haven't had a roast in a long time. Thank you for dinner, Annie."

"You're welcome," she says. "When you're done later and are up for dessert, Emma baked a blueberry pie."

He looks in my direction, and there goes my heart, fluttering in my chest.

I smile. "I made it as a celebration for you moving in."

He returns a smile, and I'm sure my heart is not going to be able to take it as it skips a beat. "Thank you."

I take a bite of the beef. But if I'm being honest, these butterflies in my stomach aren't making it possible for me to eat.

This feeling reminds me of when I first started crushing on Dean. Now, I'm crushing on someone else, and the whole feeling scares me. But I shouldn't be scared. This is the start of maybe moving on.

Chapter 12

Beck

If I die, I want my last meal to be one of Emma's pies. I don't know what she does to make them so good, but the blueberry pie tasted so much better than any pie I have ever tasted in my life.

After dinner, I offer to wash up, but Annie only shoos me away, saying there is no need for me to wash up on my first night here.

While Emma and Annie do the dishes, I decide to sit out on the veranda. Jessie follows me out and lies down next to the porch swing. In the distance, I see dark clouds moving in and wonder if that is the storm Annie said we might be getting tonight. The sun is starting to set, a light orange, pink and red in the sky. Since getting out of jail, I try to catch the sunset whenever I can. I find it's always the perfect way for me to relax and collect my thoughts.

Sometimes I wish this was something I did while growing up. Perhaps it would have stopped me from drinking.

I think of my mother, wondering how she is and pray silently that Dad does not harm her in any way. Somehow, I'm going to save up for a place down here in Maisy Grove. I'm going to rescue my mother, bring her here so she can be safe and away from Dad. I won't let him abuse her anymore. This time, I'm going to do the right thing, and not turn to drinking for the answer. The drinking wouldn't get me anywhere or stop Dad from doing what he does.

If I do drink, I won't get behind the wheel again, not after what I did to that young boy.

The flyscreen door creaks open, and I turn to see Emma. Jessie's head perks up, and Emma kneels down to scratch behind her ears before she lays her head on the ground.

Emma stands up and turns to me, a shy smile on her face. God, she is beautiful. And that kiss earlier, I want to do it again. I would be lying if I said that the kiss didn't mean anything. I mean, I wanted it to not mean anything, but all afternoon, all I could think about was her soft lips. I wonder if she'll allow me to kiss her again.

"Hey," she says.

I return the smile, hoping it will make her a bit more comfortable. "Hey."

"Do you mind if I join you?" she gestures to the empty seat beside me.

"Of course not. Take a seat."

Emma sits down on the porch swing with me.

"Do you think we'll get a storm later?" Emma nods towards the clouds in the distance.

"Maybe. Who knows what the weather will be like these days."

"I hope so. I like storms. Especially at night. I like lying in my bed and listening to the thunder, as well as watching the lightning through my window."

I nod. "By the way, thank you for making the pie. It was delicious."

Emma smiles. "I'm glad you liked it."

"Do you think you can make a savoury one next time? A meat pie, perhaps?"

She nods. "I can do that."

We sit there in silence for a bit, unsure what to say to each other. I wonder if she is thinking about the kiss earlier. Did she like it? Did she even want it? After all, she probably hasn't been with another guy since her boyfriend, and I don't want to make her feel like she needed to be in a relationship now because of it.

Not that I want a relationship. I'm still deciding on what I feel. All I know is, whenever I'm around her, my heart leaps out of my chest.

"I talked to Darcy earlier," I say.

Emma turns to me. "Yeah? What did she say? Or what did you say to her?"

"I told her that I'm your boyfriend. She doesn't believe me, though."

"Of course she doesn't. We aren't really together."

My heart crumbles in my chest.

"I know. She says you haven't been with a guy since they started working here, and they've tried to set you up with someone, but you always deny them. I told her, 'Now you know why she declined your offers, because she is with me'."

Emma laughs, which causes my stomach to do a somersault. "And what did she say to that?"

"Nothing. All she told me is to be careful of you because you're weird, and you go off at everyone. I also told her to stop putting you down. She reckons she doesn't."

"Of course she would say that. Well, thank you for helping me out. I hope they do leave me alone like you said they will."

"I can guarantee they will. They'll probably want all of the gossip about us."

Emma shakes her head. "There won't be any gossip for them."

We rock back and forth on the porch swing slowly, silence falling between us again until Emma speaks.

"Beck?"

"Yeah?"

"Do you believe Darcy? About me being weird? Am I weird to you?"

I stare at her for a long time. Each time my eyes land on her lips, I just want to lean down and kiss her. But I control myself the best I can. I don't want Emma to think I'm coming on to her.

I turn on the seat so my body is fully facing her. "No. I don't think you're weird." I push her blonde hair away from her face and tuck it behind her ear. I then let my fingers linger on her jaw. "I think you're beautiful."

Emma blushes, a smile curling across her lips. "Thank you."

I stroke my fingers against her jaw before moving them to her cheek. Her skin is so soft. Emma watches me, and soon she is leaning closer. I do the same, but before our lips touch, Emma pulls away and abruptly stands up.

"Sorry. I need to go."

She starts heading down the steps.

I get up and stand at the steps. Damn it. I've scared her off. Nice one, Beck. "Emma."

She turns to face me.

"I'm sorry," I say. "I didn't mean to upset you."

"You didn't. I have to go. I'll see you tomorrow. Good night."

"Good night, Emma."

Without another word, Emma heads back to the guest house. I watch her until she disappears inside then turn to Jessie, who is now sitting up straight.

"Do you understand, Emma?" I ask her.

Jessie barks in response.

"Do you think you can talk to her for me? Get her to open up to me?"

Jessie barks again.

"Come on, let's go on inside."

The next morning, I spring out of bed, hoping to see Emma for breakfast, but my heart sinks when I see only Annie standing at the stove, cooking eggs and bacon. Jessie spots me and strolls over, wagging her tail. I kneel down and scratch behind her ears.

"Is Emma joining us for breakfast?" I ask.

"Not this morning. Emma usually has lunch and dinner here and breakfast in her own place."

I try not to show my disappointment.

"Beck, after breakfast, all you need to do is make sure the animals have enough food and water for the rest of the day," Annie says. "As it's Sunday, I'll let you have the day off."

I smile at her. "That sounds great, Annie. Thank you."

I finish up, clear my plate and head to my room. I should call Mum to let her know how I'm doing here, but the more I think about it, the more I decide against it. It wouldn't be a good idea. If Dad's around, she won't be able to talk. I'll have to call her tomorrow when she's at work. She'll be able to talk then. Maybe I should even invite her over sometime and introduce her to Annie and Emma.

Once I head outside, I do my rounds to feed the animals. And all of which cooperate with me until I reach the goat pen, which I decided to do last.

As soon as I make my way towards the goat pen, Buckley's eyes are already on me. He narrows them.

"Okay, Buckley, are you going to let me in?"

Buckley baas, and I know he isn't going to let me in. I open the gate and step inside but can only take a couple of steps before he comes charging towards me. I hurry out of the pen and close the gate just in time. Buckley rams his head into it, and I can't help but laugh.

"Missed me." I stick out my tongue at Buckley.

Buckley stares at me for a moment before turning his back to me.

"Teasing a goat?" Emma's voice comes from behind me. I turn to see her walking over to me with a smile on her face. "That's real mature, Beck."

I look at her, innocently. "What?" I point to Buckley, who is now facing me again. "He started it."

Emma laughs. She kneels down beside the fence, and Buckley comes up to her, as well as a black and white goat, trying to get her attention. "Buckley, how many times do Annie and I have to tell you to be nice to any guys who come near the pen?"

Buckley baas, looking away.

"Do you want food, Buckley?"

At the mention of food, he turns to Emma.

"You can only get food if you let Beck in." Emma stands up and grabs a handful of feed from the bucket I'm holding. "When I get

Buckley's attention with the food, you go in. Fast. I don't know how long I can hold Buckley's attention."

I nod, watching Emma kneel down at the fence.

"Look what I have for you, Buckley." Emma places her hand through the fence. Buckley sees the food and goes for it, along with the black and white goat, both of them eating out of her hand.

With Buckley distracted, I open the gate, carefully close it behind me and make a mad dash to the food tray. The other goats follow me and watch as I pour the bucket of feed into it. Over my shoulder, I see that Buckley is almost done with his food, so I make my way back to the gate, but it's too late. Buckley turns around and spots me. Our eyes meet from across the pen.

I make a move towards the gate, and when I do, Buckley charges towards me. I curse. Emma is standing there, laughing. I make it to the gate, but I don't open it in time. Buckley rams his head into the back of my knee, knocking me to the ground. He goes to ram me again, but Emma calls him. Buckley turns to her for a moment, and with her distracting him, I manage to get to my feet and jump over the gate instead

Buckley soon realises that I have escaped and he stares me down, not daring to take his eyes off me, ready to charge at me again if I make any wrong or sudden movements.

"I can't believe Buckley did that!" Emma laughs hard.

I arch my eyebrows at her. "Oh, you think that's funny?"

Emma nods, laughter in her voice as she speaks. "I do." But then she calms down, speaking with a more serious tone. "I'm sorry. I probably shouldn't be laughing at that. Buckley could have injured you. Are you okay?"

I rub my leg where the goat had rammed me. "It's okay. A little sore, but I'm sure it's no big deal."

Emma reaches out and takes my hand. "Come inside. I'll get some ice for it."

"I'm sure it will be fine, Emma."

"Let's put some ice on it anyway."

I nod, put the bucket down and then follow Emma inside the guest house.

I glance around the living room. To the left, there's the kitchen and dining room, while there are two other doors to the right, which must be the bathroom and bedroom. The place is beautifully decorated, lots of artificial flowers in vases, and photographs of Emma and another guy. I can't see them properly from where I'm standing, but my guess is that it's her boyfriend who had died.

"Just sit down on the couch," Emma points towards the two-seated brown couch with colourful cushions.

Emma leaves the lounge room and walks to the kitchen. I sit down on the couch, waiting for her.

"Where does it hurt?" Emma asks, back with a bag of frozen peas wrapped in a paper towel.

I point to the side of my knee. "Buckley rammed me here."

"Okay, roll up your jeans."

As I attempt to, I soon realise that my jeans only roll up as far as my calves. I needed to take off my jeans for this. I warn Emma I was going to take them off. I stand up, unbuckling my belt. Emma stands there, trying not to look at me, but I can see her blushing. I chuckle.

"No need to be embarrassed," I tell Emma, pulling my jeans down and sitting back down on the couch.

"I'm not embarrassed," she says, sitting down across from me on the coffee table and placing the frozen bag on my knee. I shiver as the paper towel touches my skin.

"You're blushing, Emma."

"No, I'm not. Um, does that feel better?"

I nod, resting my hand over hers that holds the frozen bag against my skin. "It does. Thank you for doing this. I mean, I'm sure I'll be alright without the ice."

"I just want to make sure you are okay."

"I am. Thank you."

"I'm really sorry about Buckley."

"No need to apologise. That goat has issues."

Emma laughs, and my stomach flips at the sound of it.

Emma and I hold our gaze for what seems like a long time. She is the first to look away before standing up.

"Would you like a drink?" Emma starts to move away.

I reach up and grab her wrist before she leaves, removing the ice bag and setting it down on the coffee table.

"Beck, what are you doing?" she asks. "You need to keep that on for at least twenty minutes."

I pull her down onto the couch with me. "Emma, I'm fine. Really."

"I really think you need to put the ice on."

I rest my hand on her jaw. I didn't care about the ice.

She doesn't move as I tilt my head towards her, our lips touching.

Chapter 13

Emma

A million things run through my mind as Beck kisses me. I tell myself that this is what I want, but there's that guilty voice in the back of my mind, telling me that I'm cheating on Dean. But, with all the strength I can muster, I ignore the voice and kiss Beck back.

The kiss is different from our first. I climb onto his lap and wrap my arms around his neck as Beck rests his hands on my waist, holding me in place. Kissing him leaves me with an exciting feeling I never felt before with Dean. Beck moves his lips down to my neck and finds my sweet spot. I moan softly as he gently bites down on my skin.

Our lips meet again, and for a moment, I'm so lost in the kiss that I don't even remember us moving from the couch to the bedroom. Beck gently lays me down on the bed before he climbs on top of me, taking off his shirt. He kisses me again while working his fingers to open up the buttons of my plaid shirt, and I take it off once he has them undone, tossing it somewhere in my room.

As Beck moves his hands around to my back to unclip my bra, the voice is back, screaming at me for being with another man.

Beck removes my bra, moving his lips to my collarbone before making his way down to my breast when I push against his chest.

"Beck, stop," I tell him.

He listens, his eyes gazing at me. "Are you okay, Emma?"

"I'm sorry, but I can't do this."

I push him off me, and he sits aside. I sit up, covering my chest with my arms, turning my back to him. Tears fill my eyes, and I blink them away before Beck can see them.

"Emma, what's wrong?" Beck asks me. "Did I go too fast for you? I'm sorry. I should have asked."

I shake my head and turn around to face him. "No, it's not you, Beck."

Beck nods, his Adam's apple bobbing as he swallows. "It's your boyfriend, isn't it?"

I nod. "Yes. When I'm with you, I feel like I'm cheating on him even though he died two years ago."

Beck moves closer to me and rests a hand on my cheek. "Hey, it's okay, Emma. You aren't cheating on anyone."

"I don't know how to let go of him. How do you let go of someone you love so much?"

"I've never lost someone, but I can imagine the pain you feel. Emma, letting go and moving on is the hardest thing ever. Sometimes we just need to find something that will help us move on. If you let me, I can be the one to help you. Let me in, and together we can work through this."

I wasn't sure. I honestly didn't think I was ever going to meet another person after Dean passed away. And here's Beck, sitting right in front of me. He had a loving and caring personality, and he worked hard on the farm. He took the time to listen to me, and that's what I like about him. Being with him, I'm experiencing things that I haven't experienced in a long time, and maybe never experienced

"If it's okay to ask … what happened to Dean?" Beck asks. "How did he die?"

I look away, not sure if I want to tell him. I don't know Beck well enough to share this detail of my life. I can't even talk to my family or friends about it because of the painful memories it gives me. But I take a breath, and I try.

"Dean and I were in a car accident," I explain. "It happened on the night of our Year Twelve formal. We were heading home when it happened. A drunk driver slammed into us. Dean was killed instantly from the head-on collision."

As soon as I say the words, it's as if a weight is lifted off my shoulders.

Beck stares at me for a long time, processing my words. "I'm sorry about Dean."

"I can't talk to anyone about it because it leaves painful memories."

Beck reaches out to touch a strand of my hair. "Hey, I'm glad you told me. I want you to know that you can talk to me about anything. Don't be afraid. I'm here if you want to listen."

I smile at Beck and then wrap my arms around his neck. He wraps his arms around me, pulling me closer to him, rubbing a hand up and down my back.

"It's okay, Emma."

I pull away from him. "I like you, Beck. But I don't know how to move on after losing Dean. When he isn't with me, I feel lost, and I feel like if I do move on, I'll forget about him."

"You aren't going to forget him. And I understand if you want to take it slow with me."

I nod. "Yeah, that would be good."

Beck gets off the bed and looks for his T-shirt. As soon as he moves away from me, I feel my body craving him again. I want to hold him, feel him close to me. When he's with me, I feel safe, the same way Dean had always made me feel. While we were kissing, for a moment, I felt happy. Until my brain told me that I was making a mistake and that I was cheating on Dean. It's crazy to let myself think that for a second because I know I'm not.

Beck finds his shirt on the floor, but before he puts it on, I get off the bed and stand in front of him. He stares back at me, waiting to see what I'm going to do next. In my head, I can hear Daniel and Annie telling me how important it is for me to move on, Annie's wise words telling me that when I am ready, I'll be able to do just that. Am I ready to move on? How will I know when I'm ready to do that? Since Beck came here, I have never given a thought to anyone else. I never even looked at another guy before.

I remove my arms from around my chest, and I can see Beck's eyes moving down, holding his breath. He forces his eyes back up to mine.

I wrap my arms around him, resting my head on his chest as he wraps his arms around me, pulling me in close.

"When you started working here this week, I've been feeling things that I haven't felt in a long time since Dean," I admit to him. "The feeling scares me."

"It's okay to be scared, Emma. Sometimes moving on can be scary when you've been holding onto something for a long time." Beck pulls away from me. "Come on. Get dressed. Maybe we can go down to the river. Can we take the horses?"

I shake my head. "No, Darcy and Roxanne are doing lessons today."

"Right. Well, let's go for a walk down to the river. Maybe we can go for a swim."

We both get dressed, and as Beck is walking out of the bedroom, I call him, remembering our deal. He turns to look back at me.

"Now that I've told you my secret, what's your secret?" It has been on my mind since he mentioned it, and now I get the chance to know.

He doesn't answer me at first. "I can't tell you right now, but I promise you I will."

Chapter 14

Beck

I can't tell her. I can't believe this. If she knew. If she found out. I can't tell her. Because once I do, it's over. I'll have to leave this job and the farm. She will hate me forever.

That night of the accident, I was a mess. Dad and I had gotten into an argument. I was so angry that I stormed out of the house and headed to the nearest pub, like I do every time something happens between Dad and me. I usually have a few drinks, enough to make myself drunk and then sleep it off at Chandler's, so I don't have to go home and face my jerk of a father.

Only that night I had more drinks than I should have. The things Dad had said really got to me, and I hated myself so much. There were times when I wished Dad would just kill us already so we didn't have to deal with his physical and verbal abuse. And I guess that night, I just didn't care if I collapsed dead from all of the drinking I was doing. I can't even remember how many I had, but by the time I stumbled out of the pub and into my car, I could hardly walk. I should have called Chandler to come get me, but I thought I would be okay.

I wasn't. I was all over the road. I even ran a couple of red lights because, by the time I saw them, I was too slow to react, narrowly missing the cars that were crossing. But I continued, my car drifting to the wrong side of the road as my eyes became droopy, struggling to keep my eyes open, wanting to fall asleep.

And then it happened all so fast. A pair of headlights was coming towards me, but it was too late to swerve back to the right side of the road. Our cars collided.

The next thing I remember is waking up in the hospital with two police officers. My hand was handcuffed to the bed, and one officer was standing beside the bed, the other guarding the door. They explained to me what had happened, and the first thought that ran through my mind was: *what have I done?* I was only meant to have a couple of drinks and then head to Chandler's, so I didn't have to deal with Dad for the rest of the night. Instead of making it to Chandler's, I was in the hospital after killing someone. There were two people in the other car, and only one of them didn't survive. The driver. Dean Myers.

Emma's boyfriend.

I killed her boyfriend.

I was never told what her name was. I was only given the driver's name.

And if I had known about Emma living on this farm when I applied, I most likely would have rejected the job from Annie.

Now, as Emma and I walk down to the river for a swim, I realise that I can't be with her. Nor can I tell her what I have done. I like her, and there's this chemistry between us. But once she knows I'm the driver of that other vehicle that killed her boyfriend two years ago, she will hate me. Maybe kill me herself for what I did. I could have even killed her that night, but she was lucky enough to survive. Maybe if she had been the one driving that night, it would be Dean standing here instead of Emma.

"You're awfully quiet," Emma says as we near the river. "Everything okay?"

I nod, unsure how I can keep my thoughts a secret without her ever finding out who I am. Does she know the name of the drunk driver who killed her boyfriend? I mean, I guess she would know. Or even know what I look like? I don't think I saw her in the courtrooms. She didn't look familiar. The hardest part was facing Dean's parents, confessing what I accidentally did to their son.

"Yeah, I'm okay."

"Are you sure? You haven't been saying much since we left my place."

"I just have a lot on my mind."

"Anything you want to talk about?"

I shake my head. There's no way I can talk to her about this. "I'm alright."

We reach the river, and Emma is the first one to strip off her clothes, revealing the bikini she had on the other day. I follow, taking off my shirt and leaving on just my board shorts.

I watch Emma, my breath catching in my throat. Just moments earlier, we almost had sex. It's a good thing Emma had stopped us before we went further, knowingly or not. But knowing I'm responsible for what I did to her boyfriend, there's no way she would have wanted to sleep with me.

Yet, I can't help but notice how attractive she looks, or how her body looks so damn hot in that bikini. We can never be together. We just can't. I shouldn't think about any sexual thoughts towards her. We can't be together. Not after what I did.

Emma is the first to enter the water, and I follow her in. The cool water felt refreshing after walking all the way here in the hot sun.

She knows I hold a dark secret, so I don't know how to keep my distance from Emma. I mean, I came onto her earlier. What would she think if I suddenly became distant from her? I would have to tell her everything. But I really don't want to...

We splash the water at each other and swim around for a while until we settle down and just float there in the water to talk. Emma is so gorgeous, and I can see what Dean liked about her. She may seem distance, but she was kind and caring. She had a beautiful smile that lights up her whole personality, even with the pain she keeps in her. Her blue eyes shine with happiness, and it's what breaks my heart the most. From what everyone has told me, Emma has mostly kept to herself, holding onto the memories of her dead boyfriend, unable to let go. She is never happy. I noticed on my first day. She didn't smile or show much interest in me. Then, after spending a couple of afternoons with her this week, she started to smile. She was happy again, even when she sometimes cried about her boyfriend. But whenever I'm around her, she lights up...

I can never reveal my secret. It would mean taking away that happiness from her.

And I can't do that.

"How's your leg?" Emma asks me.

"It's good. I told you I was alright and that I didn't need the ice."

"I know, but I just wanted to make sure Buckley didn't hurt you too badly."

"My leg's fine. Yeah, it hurts a bit, but it's fine now."

"That's good to know."

"You're so beautiful, Emma."

She blushes at my comment, and I move closer to her. She smiles.

For a moment, I want to forget about the fact that we can't be together. Knowing that I'm the one who has been causing her pain, maybe I can be the one to fix that and take it away.

I swim closer and pull her to me until our chests touch. I tell myself that this is wrong and that I should walk away right now. But I can't. There's something about Emma that I like.

I lean in, closing the gap between us, cupping my hands around her jaw. Her hands sit on my shoulders. As I kiss her, for a moment, I forget everything about the past. Kissing Emma each time is like we we're meeting for the first time, our past never connecting together. She is just a normal girl I met at work.

After the kiss, I rest my head against her forehead, and she wraps her arms around my neck.

"I really like you, Emma," I confessed.

She doesn't say anything for a moment. "I like you too. I have never liked anyone since I lost Dean."

As soon as Emma mentions his name, I'm reminded of why I can't be with her. My stomach feels like someone has punched me. Emma may say she likes me right now, but as soon as she finds out who I really am, she isn't going want anything to do with me. I have the chance to walk away right now, tell her I only want to be friends, or better yet, tell her I don't want to talk to her ever again. But that's the thing: I will have to leave this job and this place because Emma will probably make sure I leave.

How can I walk away from her? I don't know how to.

We stay at the river for a little while before heading back to the farm. Again, I'm quiet for most of the way, thinking about everything that happened two years ago. I want to hope that Emma can forgive me and give me a chance, but I know asking for forgiveness from her is never going to happen. She must have no idea of who I am. Never heard my name or seen my face before this week. It makes me wonder how much time I have left before she does.

I walk Emma to her guest house.

"Are you sure your leg is okay?" Emma asks me for what I think is the third time.

"I'm fine, really," I answer. "Hey, about today, I didn't come onto you too fast, did I?"

Emma bites her lip. "Maybe a little. I mean, I'm not the kind of person who kisses a guy and then jumps into bed straight away with them. But, we're taking this slowly now, right?"

"Of course. I don't want you to feel that I'm pushing you to do something you don't want to do."

Emma smiles. "Thank you, Beck. I guess I'll see you later at dinner."

"You aren't coming in for lunch?"

She shakes her head. "No. I have some things to do."

"Alright, well, I'll see you later then."

Emma and I say goodbye. I kiss her one last time before she disappears inside her house. The whole time I'm walking over to Annie's, I'm cursing at myself. I know the right thing to do is to tell her who I really am, but I don't know how to say it. She has been so happy for the past week. I can't take away that gorgeous smile of hers.

I head to my room and pull out my phone.

"Chandler, I don't know what to do," I tell Chandler as soon as he picks up the phone.

"Do what, man?"

"Emma. She's the girl who was in the car that I hit. I killed her boyfriend."

Chandler curses. "Does she know who you are?"

I shake my head. "I don't think so. The worst part is that I really like her. We almost had sex today."

"Wait, what? You guys almost had sex? Mate, you have only been there for a week!"

"I know. I'm stupid. I'm so damn stupid. I'm not even sure what happened. We kissed, and I don't know, but we ended up in her room. She stopped me before we could go all the way."

"Damn, man. So, does she like you too?"

"She does, but I doubt she will like me for long when she finds out who I really am."

"Are you going to tell her?"

I sit there for a moment. Should I tell her, or should I keep it quiet, pretend I'm just someone she has met and not someone who crashed into her boyfriend's car two years ago? But who am I kidding? I can't keep this a secret forever. Somehow, she will eventually know, and I want her to hear it from me instead of someone else.

That is, if I ever gain the courage to tell her.

"If I tell her, it may mean I have to quit this job," I answer. "She isn't going to want me to be here."

"Does she really need to know? I mean, if she doesn't know that you're the person who ran into her boyfriend's car, then that's good. Just pretend the accident didn't happen."

"*But it did happen*, Chandler. I think about that night every day, wishing I could go back and change everything. Maybe if Emma hadn't told me what had happened, everything would be okay, but she told me. And now I hate myself even more because I really like her. Yet, I don't think we can be together."

Chandler is silent for a while, and I think the phone disconnected, but then he spoke. "You're right. It did happen, and you have to tell her it was you. If you're lucky, man, maybe she will forgive you. She is going to be hurt at first, but she might forgive you. You never know what could happen."

Chandler's right. I never know what could happen. Maybe Emma will forgive me. Maybe she won't. But the way she is now whenever you talk about her boyfriend, I doubt telling her what I did will end well. I know for sure she isn't going to want to have anything to do with me.

And I hate the idea of her breaking down over the news.

The right thing to do would be to tell her, but I don't know how to. It's bad enough that everyone in my hometown looks down on me. No one in Maisy Grove knows me. I wanted to start fresh here without having to walk down the street and have people whisper behind my back.

After getting off the phone with Chandler, I decide to call my mother. Annie hasn't made lunch yet, and I think maybe I can meet Mum. I'm sure she's someone I can talk to about this. If there's anyone who will understand, it's her.

She answers on the fourth ring.

"Hey, Mum," I greet her. "Is it a good time to talk?"

"Yes, your father ducked down to the servo to get cigarettes."

Good. That means Mum can get out of the house without that bastard questioning her where she is going.

"Do you want to come down to Maisy Grove? We could get lunch in town."

Chapter 15

Beck

As soon as Mum pulls up into the driveway, I know something has happened. It's thirty degrees outside, and she's wearing long sleeves.

"What did he do to you?" I get into the front passenger seat.

Mum doesn't look at me. "How's the new place going? Are you liking it here?"

"Don't change the subject, Mum. What did Dad do to you?"

Mum shifts the gear to reverse before shifting it back to drive and heads down the driveway towards the main road.

"We just got into an argument, Beck," she says, her eyes on the road. "Nothing major."

She slows to a stop, putting her foot on the brake and pulls the sleeve of her right arm up. Above her wrist is a huge bruise the size of a handprint. She pulls the sleeve back down and begins moving again.

I clench my fist in my lap. "Nothing major? Mum, he grabbed you! He could have broken your wrist or done something else."

"Honey, please. Let's not discuss this right now."

Mum reaches the end of the driveway and turns left off the main road that leads into the town.

Once I save enough money, I need to get a place here in Maisy Grove, far away so Dad can never find any of us. I'm not going to let that bastard hurt Mum any more.

"We need to discuss it," I tell her. "It's getting out of hand. What if Dad does something really bad?"

Mum gives me a small smile before turning back to the road. "Everything is okay, honey. Let's not talk anymore about this and find somewhere to eat."

I reluctantly nod, glancing out the window because of course Mum doesn't want to discuss Dad. She never does. This is probably why she never got help or why she is still living at home with him. She isn't coming forward to admit to someone that she needs help, that she needs to get away from Dad before he does something terrible.

Mum drives through Maisy Grove, looking around for a parking space. Once she finds one, we get out and look around. I haven't gotten the chance to come into town since I started working down here. I guess that's the downside of not having a car. I can't leave the property unless Annie or Emma are the ones who drive me. We walk past the pie shop where Emma told me she worked, and I'm tempted to go inside and grab a pie. But I want the first time I go there to be when she's working.

We find a cosy café just a few metres down from the pie shop and sit at a table in the back corner.

"Mum, can I talk to you about something?" I ask her once the waitress leaves with our orders.

She turns to me and smiles. "Sure you can. What's on your mind?"

"There's this girl I met. I really like her."

"Oh, you met a girl? Beck, honey, that's great. What's her name?"

"Emma. And it isn't so great. Mum, she is the girl who survived the accident. I killed her boyfriend. She lives in the guest house at Annie's farm."

Mum sits there in silence, taking in what I have said. "Does she know who you are?"

I shake my head. "No, she doesn't. At least, I don't think so. She acts like she has no idea who I am."

"You need to tell her, Beck. I know you may not want to, but you need to. She has the right to know."

Mum is right. I need to tell her. But still, I want to somehow get away with it all and not let her know. Could it be possible for me to keep this secret from her?

"If I tell her, she will hate me. She may even demand Annie to let me go. Mum, I need this job. I don't want to lose it because of my past mistakes. She is never going to forgive me for what I did. She hasn't even been able to move on."

Mum doesn't say anything to me straight away. She nods, taking in what I have said. Before she can say anything, the waitress comes over to us with our drinks, setting the two glasses of Coke down in front of us. We thank her, and she walks off. I take a sip of my drink, watching my mother, who stirs her straw around her glass.

"I know this job means something to you," Mum says. "But this girl needs to know who you are. If you want to be in a relationship with her, you need to tell her the truth. Yes, she is going to hate you. But perhaps she may forgive you. I can't really tell you what her actions will be. You can also talk with Annie, tell her what you did. And as for how Emma will react once you tell her, at least when you do tell her, and she demands that you get fired, Annie will know what's happening."

I nod. Of course telling Emma is the right thing to do. But I doubt she'll ever forgive me. And I don't ever blame her. I killed the most important person in the world to her. Now I'm stumbling into her world two years after the accident. She is unaware of who I am, but when she finds out, she'll want nothing to do with me.

"I like her, Mum. How can I like her or expect her to like me back after what I did? It feels like I'm trying to make up for what I did."

"Well, explain to her that's not what you're doing."

How could my mother sit there and give me advice but not take others' advice on leaving Dad?

"I doubt that's going to be easy."

"It won't be easy. She may not even want to hear what you have to say. But the right thing to do is to tell her."

The right thing to do is to tell her. How can I do that when I'm terrified of what she is going to say and do? I don't want to see her break down into pieces once I tell her. I can't bear to see her do that.

Chapter 16

Emma

I can't remember when I last spoke to my friends. Months ago, I think. Sometimes I received messages from them, asking me how I am, but I leave them unanswered. I see them online and what they get up to, but rarely update them on my own life. Since the night of the formal, this guy my friend Katie had been crushing on for a long time had asked her to dance that night, and the two of them have been dating since. Sammy, on the other hand, had broken up with the boyfriend she had been dating since Year Twelve. She has been dating on and off with guys but hasn't been able to be in a long-term relationship. It seemed like everyone was living their life, but me. I rather lie low so I don't have to talk about Dean.

It has been a few days since Beck and I kissed. My mind is still swirling with all kind of emotions, and I struggle to hold onto how I'm supposed to feel. There's Dean at the back of my mind, telling me to let go, but I'm still holding onto him as I explore my feelings with Beck. Thursday evening, I sit on the couch with a cup of tea and log onto Facebook. I open the group chat between my friends and me. The chat was mainly between Katie and Sammy, as I remain silent in the chat. The last message was from three weeks ago. This time, it was my turn to break the silence.

Emma: I met someone this week. Someone I think I like.

I'm hoping none of them answer straight away, that maybe I'll have some time to myself before I had to answer anything. But no, my friends are both online, and they see my message.

Katie: Emma! Hi! It's so good to hear from you!
Sammy: Wait, what? You met someone? Details!
Katie: Tell us everything!

I start typing and explaining the situation with Beck, but I don't get to fully type up the message when a video call comes up from Katie. I accept. When I do, I see both Sammy's and Katie's faces on the screen.

"Tell us everything, Emma!" Katie says. "Who's the guy?"

I laugh, remembering the times when we were in high school, how they tried to get me to spill every detail on Dean when we first started dating.

"Hello to you too," I say.

My friends greet me back, but there is no 'how are you'. It's all 'give me the details'.

"His name is Beck," I say. "He started working here on the farm. He has only been here for a week, but we have been hanging out, and he reminds me of Dean a little. I think I really like him."

Katie squeals. "Oh my gosh, I'm so happy for you, Emma! Sammy and I have always hoped you would meet someone. So tell us, is he cute?"

I smile. "He's really handsome."

"Have you kissed yet?" Sammy wants to know.

I tell them everything they want to know about the kiss and how I really feel about him. I'm not sure whether to be scared or excited, but I honestly never thought I would meet someone else after Dean.

A text comes up on my screen, a message from Kristy. I catch a glimpse of her message before it disappears. I chat with my friends a little while longer before hanging up and answering Kristy's text.

Hey, Emma, just checking up to see how you are. I have work off tomorrow, and I was wondering if you would like to catch up? Maybe we could grab some lunch.

I stare at my phone, unsure of what I want to do. Driving to Middleton was not something I had plans for on my day off tomorrow, but perhaps having lunch with my soon-to-be-sister-in-law would be good.

I texted her back and said that I would love to, even though I'd much rather stay here tomorrow. Maybe I'll take Blondie out for a ride in the morning before I have to meet up with Kristy.

I really want to take Blondie for a ride, and I want Beck to come with me, but he's working. I think of asking Annie if he could come with me, but I know she won't let him until it's his lunch break. He gets half an hour for his break, but it won't be enough to saddle up the horses and then walk the horses to a location and then come back again. And with riding lessons on this afternoon, I can't take the horses for an evening stroll.

Maybe I'll see if Beck can sneak away from his work for a while.

Beck is in the stables when I walk in there to grab Blondie's saddle from the tack room. He's carrying a bucket of water and smiles when he sees me.

"Good morning, beautiful." He puts the bucket down and greets me with a kiss.

"How are you this morning?" I ask, returning the smile.

"I'm good. What are you up to?"

"I'm going to take Blondie for a ride. Do you think you can sneak away for a while?"

"Sneak away? I don't know. I got a couple of chores I need to do this morning."

My smile fades, and I try not to show that I'm disappointed. Of course Beck can't sneak away. Even if Annie knows that something is going on between us and is glad I'm with someone who is making me happy, she wouldn't want Beck to abandon his work. I definitely don't want to get him in trouble.

"You know what, forget that I even asked," I say. "Of course you can't get away right now. Maybe we can go off later during your break." But I know that's not going to happen because when he has his lunch break, I will be with Kristy.

I start to move away, but Beck slips a hand around my wrist.

"Hey, I just need to get some chores around here done before I can take a break," he says. "I'll check with Annie to see if I can go for a short ride with you."

I smile, liking his suggestion. "Okay."

"You know, what could help me get the chores done faster is if you were to help me."

I raise an eyebrow. "You want me to help you?"

"If you don't mind."

"Okay, I'll help you out for a bit."

Beck pulls me close to him and kisses me softly.

"Shouldn't you be working, Beck?" Darcy says, walking into the stables.

Beck and I pull back, turning to her.

"I am. There's nothing wrong with giving my girlfriend a quick kiss," he tells her.

My heart flutters at the mention of him calling me his girlfriend. It's not something we have discussed yet, and I'm still not sure about being in a relationship with someone other than Dean.

Darcy rolls her eyes and disappears to the tack room.

When she is gone, I turn to Beck.

"Am I really your girlfriend?" I say in a soft voice so Darcy, or even Roxanne, who was probably somewhere eavesdropping, can't hear me. "I mean, I know we have kissed and almost slept with each other day, but what does that make us? Are we actually together, or are we putting on a show for Darcy and Roxanne?"

He doesn't answer me straight away, holding his hands around my waist. "Do you want us to be together?"

"I like you, but I don't know if I'm ready for another relationship."

Beck peeks over my shoulder, making sure Darcy doesn't come out. He then takes my hand and leads me outside of the stables. We lean up against the walls.

"Can I ask you something?" Beck says.

I nod. "Of course you can."

"When I decide to tell you about my secret, do you think you'll still like me?"

I look at him, puzzled, wondering why he would ask me that. "Of course I'll still like you. What kind of secret are you hiding?"

He hesitates. "I'm just not sure how to tell you yet, but I want to make sure you'll still want to be with me after I tell you."

"You can tell me, Beck. I will listen."

He shakes my head. "I can't yet. I'm ashamed of the secret, and a lot of people judge me for it, especially when they don't know what happened that day. Maybe it wasn't so much of an excuse, but still, people judge me."

I reach up and stroke his cheek. "I promise I won't judge you."

Beck doesn't look like he is convinced by my words, but he kisses me anyway, pushing me up against the wall and cupping a hand on my jaw.

"Will you be my girlfriend?" he asks. "For real. Not pretending we are together around Darcy and Roxanne. I really like you, Emma."

My heart flutters in my chest. Am I ready to be in another relationship after losing Dean? I'm not sure if it's the right thing to do. But I like Beck, even if I have only just met him and have been hanging out with him all week. There is something about him that is drawing me to him. Something that reminds me of Dean. Would I be stupid to tell him I don't want to be in a relationship right now?

And then there's both Daniel and Annie at the back of my mind, telling me how moving on is important for me.

I nod, smiling. "Yes, I'll be your girlfriend."

Beck returns the smile. He strokes my cheek and then leans in for a kiss. He kisses me deeply. The kiss scares me at first, thinking to myself that this is too fast and that I shouldn't be with him. But then my body relaxes, and I wrap my arms around his neck.

"Right, well, we'd better get to work then," he says. "Your first task is to make sure the horses have water. I'm going to go and speak to Annie about going on a ride with you."

He heads back into the stables.

I don't move straight away. Instead, I stand there with my back to the wall, touching my fingers to my lips and smiling. Maybe Beck is the one who will help me move on, just like Annie had told me there will be.

And I'm glad it's Beck.

Annie allows Beck to come out for a ride with me for a little while. We don't go far with our horses, just down to the river, where we stay for a short while before heading back. I let Beck get back to work before I head off to meet Kristy.

"How have you been doing?" Kristy asks me when I meet her outside the restaurant she suggested.

I nod. "Yeah, everything has been good."

Kristy smiles. "That's great to hear, Emma. I've been worried about you with what happened the other night during dinner. But I'm glad you're doing well." She gestures inside the building.

Kristy and I sit across from each other, silent for a moment as we study the menu.

"So, how are the wedding plans coming along?" I ask once the waiter leaves with our orders.

"Good, good. Everything is going well. I can't wait. I can't believe that in three weeks, I will be married to your brother."

"Well, I'm really glad you're going to be my sister-in-law, Kristy. Out of all the girlfriends my brother has had over the years, I'm glad it's you that he's marrying."

Kristy smiles. "Thank you, Emma. I'm really pleased to hear you say that."

"You're welcome."

"So, tell me, anything interesting happened to you this week?"

"You know nothing interesting ever happens to me."

Kristy shakes her head. "I don't believe that. Come on. What's new with you?"

I can't help but smile, thinking about Beck and everything that has happened between us since his arrival. My mind has been pulling me away from him, doing everything it can to keep me away, and not fall for him, reminding me constantly about Dean. But then my heart has been fighting for him. I'm scared to like him, yet at the same time, I can't deny how happy he's making me.

Before I get a chance to say anything, Kristy catches my smile. "You met someone, didn't you?"

"There's this new guy who started working on the farm. We've been getting along very well, and I think I like him."

Kristy smiles. "Emma, that's great! What's his name?"

"Beck."

"Why don't you invite him to the wedding?"

I shake my head. "No. I don't think he would like that."

"Why not? Come on, he can come as your guest."

"I don't think Daniel is going to like it."

"Why wouldn't Daniel like it?"

"Because he has always been overprotective of me. I mean, he didn't even like it when I first started dating Dean. You know what big brothers are like. Always thinking they can protect their little sisters from guys, not wanting them to hurt you even though you're perfectly capable of looking after yourself."

Kristy rolls her eyes. "Forget about Daniel. He can be overprotective all he wants, but I'm very sure he'll be happy about you meeting a guy you truly care about and who makes you happy. Are you happy with this guy, Emma?"

I nod, tucking a strand of my hair behind my ear. It still scares me that I'm liking someone other than Dean, and I'm finding myself thinking about him more than my own boyfriend. I know everyone says to move on, but I still don't know how I'm supposed to forget about Dean and move on with my life.

"Beck makes me feel happy," I explain. "But I'm scared to fall for him, and that's what is scaring me the most."

The waiter returns with our drinks. We thank him, and he walks away.

Kristy takes a sip of her drink. "Why does that scare you the most? Shouldn't it be a good thing that you're falling for him?"

"I'm scared of falling in love with someone who isn't Dean. I know everyone tells me to move on from his death, but the thought scares me, Kristy. I'm afraid of moving on, falling in love with someone and forgetting Dean. Since I started hanging out with Beck, I haven't thought of Dean as much as I usually do. We almost had sex the other day, and I don't know, but I kept thinking about Dean, and I felt it was wrong to be with someone else."

"Whoa, Emma. You and this guy almost had sex?"

My cheeks burn from bringing that part up. I'm glad it's Kristy because if it were Daniel, I'm sure he'd give me a lecture on how that's something I shouldn't be doing, even though he was the one sneaking behind our parents' backs and sleeping with his girlfriends. I'm twenty years old. I don't need my big brother telling me what I should and shouldn't be doing.

"Yeah, we almost did," I answer. "I couldn't go through with it. All I could think about was Dean. It was like I was cheating behind his back.

Kristy reaches across the table and takes my hand. "Hey, you aren't cheating on Dean. He's gone. He will be happy for you to meet someone else who makes you happy. And Emma, I know moving on may seem hard, but it's something we all eventually need to do to keep moving forward. It may seem hard, but you will be able to move on. Just be careful with this guy, and make sure this is what you really want."

"I feel it could be something I want. I just feel I need to take it slow."

Kristy smiles. "Taking it slow is fine. No one says you've to rush into a relationship. Only you know what is right. You liking this guy is a start. It's the first guy you have liked since the accident. Maybe you're ready to move on, but fear is what's holding you back. And it's okay if you feel a bit scared; just don't let it stop you from doing what's right."

I process what Kristy said. Am I really ready to move on, but fear was the only thing stopping me from doing so? Dean meant the world to me. Now that he's gone, am I truly ready to let go?

Chapter 17

Beck

It's hard to get through the day when the only thing on my mind is Emma. I'm not sure when she's getting back from lunch with her soon-to-be sister-in-law. While she's gone, I'm able to think about what I'm going to say to her about the accident. I run conversations in my head on what I could say, but it's harder than any conversation I've ever had to have. I've no idea how I'm going to tell her, and it has been a few days already since I spoke to Mum and Chandler. Telling Emma the truth is not going to be easy.

Will it be so bad if I don't tell her at all?

No, I need to take Mum's advice and tell her. If only it were so simple.

After eating lunch with Annie, I head back outside, walking over to the goat pen. Looking around to make sure Darcy or Roxanne or even Annie aren't nearby, I call up Chandler. He's at work, but I'm pretty sure he's on his lunch break right now. From across the pen, I lock eyes with Buckley. He watches me carefully as I wait for Chandler to pick up.

"Hey, Beck," Chandler answers.

"Hey, are you on your lunch break?"

"I am. What can I do for you, mate?"

"I don't know how to tell Emma who I am. I met up with my mum after talking with you, and she said I need to tell her. But that's the thing, Chandler. I don't know how. It has been a few days, and I still haven't told her. When I look at her, she is all happy being around me, and it breaks me to know she won't be happy once she finds out."

Chandler doesn't answer me at first. "I know how you're terrified to tell her anything, Beck, especially with how happy she has been lately. But eventually, the truth is going to come out. Either you tell her the truth now, or someone else will. You don't want someone else to tell her who you are. She'll be angrier, maybe unforgiving if someone else were to tell her."

I nod, rubbing a hand through my hair. Chandler's right, and that scenario still makes it hard to confess to her. I don't want Emma to hate me. I know I killed her boyfriend, and I regret that every day. But I wanted to make things right, yet I didn't know how to. I let out a breath. She just happened to be living on the same farm where I applied for a job. Is it all just a coincidence, or did it happen for a reason?

Whatever it is, Emma is never going to forgive me.

"How do I tell her?" A pit forms in my stomach.

"I don't know, man. You just have to sit her down and tell her. There's going to be yelling, and you will need to be prepared that she will never forgive you. Imagine being in her shoes, and someone were to run into you and kill your girlfriend, wouldn't it be hard for you to accept an apology from the person who killed her?"

I play out the scenario in my head as if it were me instead of Emma. How would I react to the person if they were the ones who had killed my girlfriend? I would be angry at the world. Perhaps even at myself because I couldn't do anything to protect her from the incident. Emma could feel the same way.

I hate myself. I shouldn't have gotten into the car that night. I was too intoxicated and angry with my dad. The alcohol was the only thing that comforted me, and look where it had gotten me that night. I should have been the one to die that night, not Dean. I took away his life because of my stupid decision.

After thanking Chandler for the advice, I hang up the phone and just stand there, resting my phone against my chin, lost in my thoughts. How do I tell her?

"Is everything alright, Beck?"

I turn to see Annie, walking closer to me. Did she hear everything I said to Chandler?

"Yeah, I'm fine, Annie. I've just got a lot on my mind."

"Anything you want to talk about?"

I don't want to get into a full conversation with Annie about my past. She knows I have been in jail, but never asked more about it.

"How would you tell someone about something that happened in the past?" I ask her. "Something that connects you to that person, in something you know they may never forgive you for, and you really don't want to tell them because you don't want to see them get hurt?"

Annie studies me for a second. "Is this about Emma?"

On her name, it's as if my heart has been pierced with a knife.

"I did something really terrible in the past." I don't mention it's about Emma, but maybe Annie will connect the dots somehow. "Now, I've come across this one person who was there when I made the mistake. They have no idea who I am or that I am the one who caused the accident, and I don't know how to tell them what I did."

Annie nods slowly. "I see. This would be something difficult to tell that person. I know it's hard, but you just need to figure out how you are going to say it and then say it to them. I can understand if you never want to mention it to them, but the secrets always come out in the end, Beck. It's either you tell them now, or they will find out sooner or later. It's also better for it to come from you. You don't want someone else to tell them or for them to discover the secret first. Whatever you did, that person may be mad, but they will be madder if you never tell them straight away, especially if they find out in an unexpected way that isn't coming from you."

I take in everything Annie tells me. She's saying the exact same thing as my mother and Chandler. I have to tell Emma, but I don't know how I'm going to do that yet.

And when I do tell her, she may never speak to me again.

"Emma, there's something I need to tell you. I'm the one who killed your boyfriend."

I shake my head at my reflection in the mirror. No, what am I thinking? I can't say that!

I've been staring at the mirror for the last fifteen minutes, trying to figure out the right wording of this confession. But so far, I haven't had any luck. I'm not getting anywhere by saying these stupid lines to the mirror. Everything I say isn't right. Everyone tells me I need to confess to Emma about what happened that night, but it's easier said than done. Coming up with the right words to say isn't easy. It doesn't matter how many times I practise in the mirror, the right words will never be enough to convince her not to hate me.

That night, I had caused so much pain to everyone. Dean's family, his friends and, of course, Emma.

How can I expect Emma to forgive me? Or how do I make up for what I have done?

I can't make up for it. The whole accident is my fault.

A knock comes on the door, startling my thoughts.

"Beck?"

I jump at the sound of her voice. I open the door, and my heart skips at the sight of her. I tell myself that I can't fall for her because once she finds out the truth, she won't want me. But I can't help but take in her beauty, her thin frame. She looked so good in the jeans shorts and flannel shirt she was wearing, her blonde hair pulled back in a ponytail. Why couldn't we just be strangers?

Hopefully she didn't hear me talking to myself. The last thing I want is for her to have heard everything I've been trying to practise.

I smile. "Hey."

She walks closer to me. "Hey, Annie said dinner is almost ready."

"Alright. I'll be out in a second."

She starts to turn, and I let out a sigh of relief. She didn't hear anything I said.

"Emma." She turns back to me. "How was your lunch with your sister-in-law?"

"Oh, she isn't my sister-in-law until next month. Lunch was good. Actually, I wanted to ask you something. Kristy suggested it, and I was wondering if you would like to come along as my date to the wedding."

If it were any other kind of situation where I wasn't keeping a horrible secret from the past, I would have jumped at the idea of saying yes. But the thought of saying yes meant meeting Emma's family. What if they know who I am? I mean, I'm sure they would know, even if Emma doesn't. And is Dean's family still close to Emma's? What if they're there? I can't bear to come face-to-face with Dean's family. I still remember their faces in the courtroom, shooting daggers with their eyes across the room, wanting me to rot in hell for taking away their son. His dad was the one I didn't want to come across. I'm sure if that dude could, he would have bashed me to death. When I was found guilty, the man spat at me when I walked past him. "Rot in hell, you son of a bitch," he told me.

The words have stuck with me since then. That night fills me with regret each day, and I would do anything to make it right. Even now, as I try to put my life back together, I'm not even sure how to cope. I have been sober for two years. Being in jail I had no choice, but every day I want to buy myself a case of beer to drown my sorrows in. Back then I promised myself that I would never drink again, but if I were to lose Emma, I don't know what I'd do.

"I'm not sure that's a great idea, Emma," I tell her.

Her face falls. "Why not?"

"Because..." I stare at her, my brain screaming at me to tell her the truth, to stop being a wuss and tell her what I'm hiding from her. "Why would they want a guy like me at the wedding and hanging out with you?"

"What do you mean, Beck? I'm sure everyone's going to love you."

No, they won't. They will tell me to stay away from you and to rot in hell.

I approach her slowly. "Emma, I was in jail. They aren't going to want me there."

"What were you in jail for?"

I killed your boyfriend. The words are on the tip of my tongue, but I can't bring myself to say them. I just can't.

I push past Emma and move over to sit down on my bed. How do I tell her?

"What did you do, Beck?" she asks me again, approaching me. "I'm sure it's nothing serious that my family and friends won't like you for. I mean, it's not like you murdered someone."

A nauseous feeling builds up in my stomach when she says it. *I killed Dean.* An innocent eighteen-year-old who had just graduated high school and was spending the night of his high school formal with his girlfriend. Emma could have been killed too, but instead, she was standing right here in front of me, completely oblivious to the fact that I'm the one who had crashed into them that night.

Spit it out, Beck.

"I was driving under the influence, and I crashed the car," I say. But still, when I look at Emma, I can't tell her the full truth. It will break her. "I crashed into a tree. I don't remember what happened. All I remember is waking up in the hospital with a police officer beside me, where he had handcuffed me to the bed."

Emma gasps, tears prickling her eyes. "How could you be so reckless, Beck? You could have killed someone! Or yourself!

I did kill someone, I wanted to say, but I can't bring myself to say the words.

I nod. "You're right. I was reckless for what I did."

Emma stands there for a moment, and I can see she is lost in thought of the memories of the accident.

I turn away from her. I can't look at the sadness in her eyes. Not what I did to her that night.

"But I'm not that reckless person anymore," I assure her, my eyes staring at the floor. "That night made me realise how irresponsible I was, and I would do anything to go back to change the night."

Emma sits down beside me, resting a hand on my shoulder. "We all make mistakes, Beck. What matters is that you're trying to move forward and make changes in yourself."

I nod. Would Emma be telling me that if she knew the actual truth?

"Beck, I'm not going to judge you. No one in my family will."

"People judge me over it. I'm an alcoholic, just like my father."

Emma rests a hand on my jaw and turns my head gently towards her. "Hey, it's okay. And if you don't want to drink at the wedding, it's fine. My family is going to love you, Beck. So far, Kristy is the only person who knows about you, and so do my friends. They're happy that I'm seeing someone, and they can't wait to meet you."

I nod, watching her carefully and trying to picture myself at the wedding ceremony. All I can think about is the judging eyes, even when Emma said everything was going to be fine. It won't be once I tell the truth.

"Emma, I..." I stop myself. How can I tell her what happened when there's hope in her eyes that I will say yes to coming to the ceremony?

Tell her, Beck. Tell her!

"I really don't think it's a good idea."

"Why not?"

"I just don't think I should."

"Beck, please. I want you to be there."

You need to tell her now, Beck.

"Okay, I'll come to the wedding with you," I answer instead of telling the truth.

Emma smiles and throws her arms around me. "Thank you, Beck. I just know everyone is going to be happy to meet you."

At the back of my mind, I know no one is going to like me. I still feel that, in some way, someone is going to recognise me and then ruin everything. I enjoy being around Emma. She has made me feel wanted, and like I could start over and not have to worry about someone judging me for my past actions. But at the same time, I know Emma and I can't be together.

"Hey," Emma rests a hand on my cheek. "Why are you so sad?"

"It's nothing, Emma."

"It is something. You can tell me. Is it the alcohol at the wedding? You don't have to drink, Beck. If it makes you feel better, I won't drink. I'm not much of a drinker anyway."

I want to tell her that the drinking isn't it. But even though I want to break the news to her about who I really am, my mouth can't say the words. Nothing comes out.

I smile at her because what else can I do? I can't bring myself to say the truth.

"Thank you, Emma. I really appreciate it."

I cup a hand on her jaw and kiss her. The hand she has resting on my cheek lingers there for a few minutes before she wraps both her arms around my neck. She moves closer to me, and I can feel the heat between our bodies, making me crazy, and all I want is to push her down onto my bed, climb on top of her and do whatever I want with her. But it is so hard to resist doing any of that, knowing fully well that I can't take advantage of her. I don't want to make her regret sleeping with me.

I pull away first before any temptation takes hold of me.

"We should head to the kitchen before Annie comes looking for us," I say.

"I'm sure she'll be okay with us staying in here for a little while longer."

"We could, but I don't know about you, I'm starving. So let's go have dinner."

Emma pecks my lips one last time and gets off my bed first, taking my hand and then pulling me off the bed. Together, we head to the kitchen.

In the back of my mind, I know I'm digging myself an even bigger hole each day for not telling Emma the truth. And I don't know how to get myself out of it.

Chapter 18

Emma

This is moving on. I'm finally doing something that everyone has wanted me to do for the past two years. I've met someone, and I'm not spending my time hung up over my former boyfriend. This man, Beck, makes me feel like it's worth moving on instead of holding myself back and wishing to go back to the past.

My friends Katie and Sammy have tried to set me up on blind dates before, hoping it would get me out of the house and give me something to look forward to. Of course, I never went out on those dates. The blind dates my friends tried to set me up on were probably better than the parties Darcy and Roxanne tried to get me to come out to and meet someone. Katie and Sammy eventually stopped trying to set me up after the third attempt, understanding that I wasn't ready to take that step yet.

Then here comes Beck, someone who has come into my life and totally changed me. When we can, each afternoon after work, we spend time with each other. Sometimes we take the horses for a ride down to the river. On the hot afternoons, we go swimming.

The one thing I'm looking forward to the most is the wedding. I can't wait for my family and friends to meet Beck. I just know they'll love him and welcome him with open arms, probably glad to meet the man who has swept me off my feet after such a long time. Daniel, I think, will have a hard time adjusting to Beck, as he always thinks he needs to be the overprotective brother. But in the end, I know he'll love Beck just as much as he loved Dean.

"What has gotten you all happy?" my co-worker Brenda asks me on Friday afternoon with a tray full of freshly made meat pies to add to the displays. She's also my boss's daughter. "I don't think I've ever seen you this happy. Who's the guy?"

"What makes you think it's a guy?" I say by the counter, waiting for the next customer to arrive.

Brenda shrugs, using a tong to gently pick up the pies and move them into the displays. "No reason. It's just that I've never seen you this happy since you started working here. So I figure it must be a guy, because with that goofy smile on your face, it's exactly how I looked when I first started dating Chad."

"I do not have a goofy smile."

She looks up at me with a smile. "Of course you do, Emma. Whenever I've caught a glimpse of you this week, I would catch this smile on your face, like you're thinking about someone. Who's the guy?"

There's no denying how I feel. "His name is Beck."

"Ooh, Beck. Tell me about him."

"Well, he started working on the farm two weeks ago, and we've been hanging out with each other. And you know how Darcy and Roxanne are always giving me a hard time for not wanting to go to parties with them and hooking up with guys?"

Brenda nods, putting the empty tray and tong down on the counter. "I do. The very same girls who always bullied me in high school. And then they bullied my cousin Kyla when she moved here, all because she was a city girl."

"Beck thought it would be a good idea to give them something to talk about in the hope they would lay off on me a little, and suggested we pretend to be together. He kissed me."

Brenda gasps. "He kissed you! What happened after that? Did his plan work?"

I roll my eyes, smiling. "Let me tell the story, and then you can ask questions."

"Right. Sorry. Continue."

"Darcy and Roxanne don't believe there's something going on between us. But what do they know? They don't know anything about me. Beck and I hang out after work and over the weekend. When it's hot, we go down to the river, and sometimes we bring the horses along." I twirl a strand of my hair around my finger, smiling as I think about those moments. "The past two years have been hard for me, and being around Beck has really made me happy."

Brenda smiles. "That's great to hear. I'm so happy for you, girl."

"Have I ever told you about my last boyfriend?"

She thinks about it for a moment and then shakes her head. "No, I don't think you even mentioned you had a boyfriend." She moves closer to me. "What happened? Did he do something to break your heart, Emma? If he did, I will kick his ass for you."

I shake my head. "There's no need for you to do that, Brenda." I look away from her. "My boyfriend actually died in a car accident we were in a couple of years ago."

"Oh, Emma." She rests a hand on my shoulder. "How come you never told me?"

"It isn't exactly something I like to talk about."

"Well, I'm all ears if you ever want to talk about it."

I smile, turning to look back at her. "Thanks. Anyway, I haven't been able to move on from his death. And then Beck came along, and I just started falling for him. I really like him."

"You should bring him around. I'd like to meet him."

"I'm sure you'll love him."

"Let him know too that if he ever breaks your heart, I'm kicking his ass."

I laugh. "You aren't kicking anyone's ass, okay? And he isn't going to break my heart."

"I just want to look out for you."

"And I appreciate that, Brenda."

She grabs the tray and tongs. "Well, I'd better bring these back. Don't daydream too much while I'm gone."

Of course when she is gone, and I'm alone in the front, tidying up the storefront and waiting for more customers, I think about Beck. I also think about what Brenda said about him breaking my heart. That's something I haven't thought of. I'm not sure that's something I can take after my heart broke once. I'm falling for Beck, and I know that could be a bad thing.

But I'm sure whatever fears I have, they're just stopping me from moving on. Life goes on after someone dies, and I need to move along with life. And Beck is helping me to do just that.

Chapter 19

Beck

Dad is calling me.

I'm frozen still, watching the screen of my phone light up with a name I never thought I'd see there again. Dad. The one person I never want to speak to ever again for as long as I live.

I decline the call and go back to sprinkling the chicken feed on the ground. The chickens gather around me, pecking at their food. Across the chicken coop, I see Buckley still staring me down from his pen, like he was warning me not to come any closer to the fence.

Rejecting Dad's call was a waste of time because the jerk only called again.

Might as well as see what the jerk wants from me.

"What do you want?" I answer. I haven't seen him since I was sent to jail. The bastard never came to visit me. Actually, I didn't allow him to come visit me. I didn't want him there. I only ask Mum, Chandler and Lisa to visit me.

"Well, that's not the way you greet your father."

"Yeah, well, you aren't much of a father anyway."

"Doesn't matter if I don't act like much of a father. I'm still your father. It has been nearly a month, Beck. How do you think it makes me feel that you contact your mother, but you can't contact me to see how I'm doing?"

I frown. Is he kidding me? Does he really expect me to talk to him after he was the reason why I drank and made a stupid decision? I rather disowned him as my father.

"Yeah, well, you aren't exactly the kind of person I want to talk to," I tell him.

"Still blaming me for the reason why you got drunk and killed the driver?" He chuckles. "Oh, Beck. It wasn't me who caused you to do those things. It was all you. You are the one who drank so much and then got behind the wheel. Don't blame me for anything."

Of course Dad doesn't want to take the blame for anything. I mean, yeah, he's right about me drinking too much and then getting behind the wheel. It was my decision to do so. But he was the reason why I was drinking. If we hadn't argued that night, maybe I wouldn't have gone to the pub.

"What do you want, Dad?" I ask, so badly wanting to hang up the phone and continue with the rest of my day.

"I want you to come see me," he says.

At this, I burst out laughing. "You want to see me? What for, Dad? So you can verbally abuse me, make me go back to my old habits and land myself back in jail?" I shake my head. "No. I'm not seeing you. I don't want to ever see you again for as long as I live."

I imagine Dad frowning on the other end of the line, and I was thankful I was saying this over the phone. If I weren't and I were standing right in front of him, he would have punched me in the face.

"You can see your mother, but you can't see me. How do you think that makes me feel, son? If you don't come to see me, I'll hurt your mother. Maybe that'll change your mind."

I clench my free hand into a fist. I can hear the evil tone in his voice as he says this, reminding me that he has the power to control my mother and me. He has the final say, even if we don't agree to it. And he wasn't kidding. He really will hurt my mother if I don't obey him.

"There's no reason for you to hurt her," I tell him. "I will come to meet you."

"Good. Meet me at Middleton Hotel. I'll buy you a beer."

The thought of going to a pub and being surrounded by people who are drinking makes me uncomfortable. It's not a place I want to be if I want to change my habits.

"Thanks, Dad, but I don't drink anymore."

Dad gives a mocking laugh. "You don't drink anymore? Trying to be a good little boy after you got out of jail? Afraid of having one little sip of beer?"

"One beer can lead to many more. I'm done with drinking, Dad. I'm not going to drink the way I did and kill someone else, or even myself. I'm not going to jail again."

"Don't be a pussy, Beck. How soon can you get to the hotel?"

I pull my phone away from my ear and look at the time. It's eleven o'clock. Both Annie and Emma will be getting back from the farmer's market just after noon.

"I can do one-thirty," I say.

"One-thirty it is then. I'll see you then, son."

He hangs up. "Bastard," I mumble. Why is he doing this to me? What is the real reason he wants to see me? What is he trying to do? Hoping I mess up and go to jail again? No. I'm not going to do that. I'm not going to touch the beer. I know that if I take one sip of the drink, I'll only go for another, especially while he throws insults at me. I'm going to be stronger than before. I'm not going to let him think he can tear me down. I'm going to be strong and not turn to alcohol when I'm down.

I slip the phone back into my pocket and go back to work. The goats are next, and right now, I don't really want to deal with Buckley. Emma or Annie isn't here to distract him, so I'm truly on my own with him.

I walk over to his pen, one hand on the gate, the other holding a bucket full of food. Buckley stares at me from across the pen, narrowing his eyes at me as he usually does, ready to come charging at me once I open the gate.

In one swift motion, I unlock the gate, quickly closing it so no goats can escape. Buckley charges at me, and I make a mad dash across the pen to the grain feeder. The other goats see me with the food and begin following me. I make it to the grain feeder and pour the feed into it as Buckley is right at my side. I make a run for the exit. The other goats start eating, but Buckley's eyes are still on me, following me across the pen once more, making sure I don't come back. Later, I need to come back in here with some hay, but I'm not sure how I'm going to do that. Maybe Annie or Emma will do that once they get here.

I open the gate and make it out just in time, closing it behind me. Buckley stares and baas at me to stay out of the pen.

"Come on, Buckley, we should be pals by now," I say to him. "Don't you want to like me? We could be great friends. How else am I supposed to feed you and the others if you don't like me being in the pen?"

He baas again before turning his back to me and joins the others at the grain feeder.

"I'll be back again, Buckley, with some hay," I call out to him.

With the chickens and goats both fed, I head towards the stables, checking to see how the horses are. There are a few children around, preparing for their riding lessons with Roxanne and Darcy. I do my best not to run into them, because the last thing I want is to run into them and get bombarded with questions about my relationship with Emma.

Avoiding them isn't easy.

Darcy spots me and makes her way over to me.

"Anything I can help you with, Beck?" she asks with a smile.

"Just checking the horses are all good."

Darcy nods. "They are fine. The children are almost done with setting the horses up for riding."

"Great, well, I'll be around, so let me know if you need anything."

I turn to leave, but Darcy grabs my arm. Her hand moves its way up to my bicep.

"Hey, I was wondering, when Roxanne and I finish up here for the day, maybe you would like to come out with us and get a drink?"

I frown at her, shaking her hand off me. First my dad wants me to come out for a drink, and now Darcy does too. "No, thanks. I don't drink."

"What do you mean you don't drink?" she asks me, confused. "Everybody drinks."

"I don't. Excuse me, I have to go and do a few things around the farm."

I leave before she can stop me again. I glance at my phone. It's almost noon, which means Annie and Emma will be returning home soon. My heart does a flip when I think of Emma. I still yell at myself for not telling her the truth about who I really am, and I still haven't figured out how I'm going to tell her.

While I wait for them to arrive, I fetch some fresh hay from the barn, making my way over to the goat pen again. Buckley's eyes immediately meet mine. I grab some hay and hold it out to the goat, calling him to come over. Maybe if I can distract him with the hay, he might not notice me sneaking in. Buckley watches me, trying to decide if what I am doing is a trick. But when a few goats make their way over to me, going for the hay, he follows suit. He goes for the hay, and I manage to get in with the wheelbarrow. I spread the hay around the pen for the goats and then make my way out before Buckley sees me.

But it doesn't matter what I do because Buckley's eyes and ears are everywhere. He looks up at me after he finishes his hay and comes charging towards me, and I run to safety. I make it out of the gate in time before he can ram me with his horns.

"Missed me, Buckley." I stick out my tongue at him.

He baas at me before moving along and rejoining the other goats to eat.

I move away from the animals and clean up a bit. I almost go to the barn to check up on the horses one last time, but I stop myself, not wanting to run into Darcy again. Plus, I'm sure they've started their riding lessons, and I don't want to be in the way. Instead, I head inside to get myself a drink. Jessie's lying on the veranda and looks up at me as I walk towards her. Her tail wags faster the closer I get, and she gets to her feet, barking.

"Hello to you too, Jessie."

I scratch behind her ears and then head inside. She follows me. I grab a glass from the cabinet and fill it with water and stare out the window as I drink, keeping a look out for Annie's truck, which should pull up very soon.

"I'm surprised you're meeting up with your dad," Emma says. "I thought you didn't get along with him."

I shake my head, keeping my eyes ahead, not wanting to glance at Emma. I don't want her to see the worry in my eyes, not knowing what will happen when I see my father soon. It's clear from our phone call that he hasn't changed. It makes me wonder what he's up to and why he wants to see me so badly. I mean, I'm sure he doesn't give a damn about me, and meeting up with him is probably an excuse for him to go out for a drink.

"I don't get along with him," I explain. "But for whatever reason, he wants to see me."

"Maybe he misses you." She glances at me briefly before turning her eyes back to the road.

I scoff. "I doubt it."

"I can stay nearby if you'd like," Emma volunteers. "That way, if something happens, we can make a quick getaway."

I think about it for a second. Originally, I thought of Emma staying in the car until I was done with Dad because I honestly doubted that I would stay for long. He'll most likely say something to piss me off, and the last thing I want is to do something stupid that could land me back in jail. Besides, it's hot out, and I don't want Emma to sit in the hot car. She might as well come inside the pub where there'll be air conditioning.

I turn to her. "I would like that. Can we go into the pub separately? I don't want my dad to see you. He isn't like one of those dads you want to introduce your girlfriend to. He's a total jerk, Emma. I don't want him to say anything nasty to you."

Emma nods. "Okay, Beck. I'll be nearby, and you let me know when you want to leave."

"Trust me, I'm sure I'll be out the door as soon as I see the jerk."

"Don't walk out the door too soon. Just go and see what he wants, and then we can leave."

"Okay."

Emma finds parking at the Middleton Hotel. For a moment, I just sit there as she unbuckles her seat belt and takes the keys out of the ignition, lost in my own thoughts. In the back of my mind, I know this is a bad idea, but at the same time, if I don't get out of this car and go in, Dad will hurt Mum.

I force myself to unbuckle my seat belt and get out of the truck before sending a quick text to my dad to let him know I'm here.

"So what's the plan?" Emma asks, coming around to my side.

I put my phone in my pocket and turn to her. "I'll go in first, and you go in next." I pull out my wallet, pulling out a twenty-dollar note and handing it to her. "Here. Go and get yourself something for lunch or a drink."

Emma doesn't take it. "Beck, really. You don't need to pay me."

"It's okay. You drove me here, and I want to give you some money for it."

Emma takes the note from me. "Thanks, Beck."

I give her a peck on her lips. "I'll see you inside."

I head on in. Rock music plays softly inside the almost-empty room. I scan the surroundings and soon spot my dad across the room, his back to the TV streaming a soccer match, already he's sipping on a glass of beer. In front of him is a second glass of beer, and my guess is it's for me. I roll my eyes at the sight.

I head over to the bar before I make my way to him, ordering myself a Coke, keeping my word about not drinking. I don't care what Dad says. He can't make me turn back to my old habits again.

I sit down across from him. As I do, I see Emma walking into the pub.

Dad frowns at me when he sees the Coke in my hand. "Seriously, Beck? I was nice enough to buy you a beer, and you get a Coke instead. Ungrateful child, you are."

I take a sip of my drink before I place it down in front of me. "First of all, I'm not a child. I'm a twenty-three-year-old man. I'm also old enough to make my own decisions. I'm no longer drinking alcohol. Not after what I did to that guy."

As soon as I mention Dean, my eyes quickly glance over at Emma, where she's ordering a drink at the bar. I'm glad she isn't near us because the last thing I want is for her to hear this conversation. I can imagine Dad loving the idea of her coming over here and yelling at me. The thought of her even finding out still haunts me, and just thinking about it makes my stomach twist into knots.

My eyes are off Dad for less a second when I hear a thump on the table. I turn to see he had purposely knocked over my glass. The Coke spills everywhere. I quickly save the rest of the drink before it all goes, only leaving me with a quarter.

"You bastard," I tell Dad. "Why would you do that?"

Dad narrows his eyes at me. "Don't use that language with me."

"What?" I ask innocently. "I can't call you a bastard, but it's alright to call your own son horrible names?"

If we weren't in a public place, Dad would have pounded me already for speaking like that to him.

"I'm your father. I can call you whatever I want."

I drink the rest of my Coke before Dad has the chance to spill the rest of it.

"So, what do you want, Dad?" I ask, putting my glass down. "You call me up and say you want to see me, but as soon as I get here, you spill my drink."

He snickers. "I wanted to see you, Beck. You refused to allow me to come to visit you in jail. Now that you're out, you still don't want to talk to me?"

I look around to see where Emma is and find her only a couple of tables away from me. I think I have about enough already and want to leave.

"You put me in jail, Dad. Why would I want you to come to visit me? So you can rub it in my face?"

Dad points his finger at me. "No. I didn't put you in jail. You put yourself there."

"But you are the one who made me get so intoxicated."

"Again. You are the one who got intoxicated. I never made you do it."

No, you are the one who made me feel so worthless that I kept drinking because I thought it would make me feel better, I want to say, but I keep that to myself. There's no use saying it out loud. Not when my own father would laugh in my face about it.

"So, are you going to ask how I am doing, or are you just going to insult me?" I say instead. "Otherwise, I'm just going to leave."

"How are you doing, Beck?" he asks me. "What have you been up to?"

"I moved out of town, and I got myself a job."

"Yeah, where did you move to and where are you working?"

"None of your business."

He leans across the table. "It is my business to know where you are at all times."

"So you can come after me when you need to take it out on me?"

Dad looks around before turning back to me. "You're really pushing your luck. If I didn't suggest for you to meet me here, I would be beating the hell out of you."

"Then hit me, Dad. Hit me right here. Come on. I dare you."

Dad snickers, shaking his head at me. "Your smart mouth has not changed one bit since you were locked up."

"Yeah, well, you know what?" I start to stand. "I think I'm going to go."

"Sit!" He gestures for me to sit back down. I do as he says. He points to the glass of beer. "Drink that."

I eye it. "No."

"Drink it, Beck. I offered to take you out for a beer, and I've bought you one, so drink it." He then leans in closer. In a lower voice, he says with an evil look in his eyes, "You don't want me to hurt your mother, do you?"

Dad and I stare at each other for what seems like a long time. He knows how to get me to do something. He always threatened to hurt my mother when I didn't want to do something.

I grab the glass and start drinking it. As soon as the bitter cold drink touches my tongue, the guilt of what I did two years ago floods me, seeing the headlights in my mind as I crash into Dean and Emma, as I sit in the courtroom, the judge displaying all of my charges to me, the torment of every day since then.

Just as I'm about to put my glass down, Dad stops me. He places his hand under the glass and tips it towards me more, with a huge grin on his face, enjoying torturing his own son.

"Good boy," he tells me. "Drink it all up, and I'll buy you another beer afterwards."

I need to get out of here. I don't want to see my father ever again. He doesn't deserve me as his son.

I push the glass away, and frown. "Are you trying to kill me? I could have choke on that!"

"You're not going to choke. Just finish the rest of it."

I shake my head. "I don't want to drink anymore."

Dad narrows his eyes. "Finish it, Beck."

I don't dare to question my dad and drink the rest of the glass. Dad's smug face watches me.

"Leave him alone!"

I look up to see Emma standing beside our table. She pours her drink on top of my father's head, making him let go of my glass. Immediately, I put the glass down and I look between Dad and Emma, seeing the fire in his eyes. Without the need to know what he's going to do with her, I grab her wrist and drag her out of the pub. We run back to the truck, Dad on our tails, yelling at us, but trips over his own feet.

We get into the truck, and Emma turns the ignition, backing out of the parking lot as fast as she can. Dad comes towards the truck, ready to jump out in front of us, but Emma manages to steer out of the way, avoiding a collision with my father, speeding off down the street. She doesn't stop, knowing that it isn't safe to do so. Dad is probably getting into his car and coming after us.

Emma drives down a couple of streets before pulling into a park when we're sure we have lost him.

Chapter 20

Emma

I look around, double-checking Beck's dad isn't following us and cut the engine. I turn to Beck, who is sitting there still, most likely in shock from what had happened back at the pub.

"I think we lost him," I say. "Are you okay, Beck?"

He turns to me. "Are you crazy?"

I stare at him wide-eyed, wondering why all of a sudden he's upset with me. He begins talking before I even have the chance to respond.

"I told you to not come anywhere near my father and me while we were together," he says.

"I'm sorry, Beck. I didn't like what he was doing to you and had to get you out of there. That's abuse what he was doing to you, Beck! You could have choked! I wasn't going to let you do that while he was forcing beer down your throat."

"You don't know my father, Emma. He could have hurt you! And I'm not going to let him or anyone hurt you. Not after what—"

He stops mid-sentence before looking away. I wait for him to continue, but he doesn't.

"Not after what, Beck?"

He shakes his head. "It's nothing."

"No, it is something. Tell me, Beck."

He turns to me, worry flickering in his eyes. There's also a hint of guilt in them, and I wonder what he's thinking about.

"You know how I drank so much once because of the argument I had with my dad?" I nod. "Well, I did something stupid afterwards, and I promised myself that I was never going to do it again. It still haunts me to this day, and I don't want to go through it again. I don't want to hurt anyone, and that includes you."

"What did you do, Beck? Tell me."

"I can't tell you."

"What do you mean you can't tell me? Of course you can."

He shakes his head. "I really can't tell you."

"Why not?"

He stares at me. "Emma, I... Let's just say it has something to do with the accident I caused when I was intoxicated. I knew it was wrong that I had gotten behind the wheel, but I did. I regret every moment, and I wish I could go back to change it all."

"Can you please tell me what you did?"

"I can't," he whispers, looking away from me.

"Why not, Beck?"

"Let's not talk about this anymore."

We sit there in silence for a moment until I reach over and rest my hand on his cheek. He reaches up and holds my wrist.

"Hey, it's okay, Beck. You don't have to tell me now. Tell me when you're ready. And there's no reason for you to worry about hurting me. You aren't going to hurt me, and your father is definitely not going to hurt me." I give him a small smile to reassure him.

He doesn't smile back. Instead, he moves my hand from his face, unbuckling his seat belt and leans towards me, cupping his hands around my jaw, and kisses me. I unbuckle my own seat belt and move my arms around his neck. Beck's lips move down to my neck.

"You know I love you, Emma?" he whispers against my neck.

Butterflies dance around my stomach. I wasn't expecting it. We haven't known each other for long, and I'm not sure if we are at the love you stage yet. Beck lifts his head to stare at me, waiting for me to respond to his comment. Do I love Beck, too? I haven't fallen in love with anyone since Dean died, and I wasn't sure if I wanted to fall in love again. But being with Beck for these past few weeks has made me feel like it's possible to fall in love again.

"I love you too, Beck," I reply.

Beck smiles and presses his lips against mine.

We make out in the car for a little while longer before we decide to head home. It isn't safe on these streets with Beck's dad roaming around, and the last thing we want is to be caught by him again.

The drive home is silent, and I'm not sure if Beck is still mad at me or if he is just lost in his own thoughts. I pull up outside Annie's home and cut the engine. As I reach for my seat belt, Beck's hand sits on mine. I look up at him; his eyes continue to swim with guilt, and I wonder what he thought about on the way home.

"I want to apologise again for raising my voice at you," he says. "I know you were trying to help. Thank you."

I stare at him, and for a moment, all I can think about is the way he kissed me, how it reminded me of the time when Dean and I were together, bringing up old feelings that I didn't think I would ever feel again.

I smile at him. "It's fine, Beck. Don't worry about it."

We get out of the car.

"Thanks again for coming along with me," Beck says, coming around to my side as I lock the door.

"You're welcome. I wish things worked out better for you and your dad."

"Same, but things will never be okay with my dad and me." He looks towards the house. "He has been abusing me since I was a child. He abuses my mum as well."

"I'm sorry to hear that. He shouldn't treat you like that."

He turns to me. "I'll see you later at dinner?"

I nod, but I don't want him to disappear just yet. I wanted to ask him more questions, but I didn't want to push him if he doesn't want to talk.

He turns to walk towards the house but stops when I call his name.

"I'm thinking of making some tea. Would you like some?"

"I don't drink tea."

"Hot chocolate then? Sorry, I don't have any coffee. Just tea and hot chocolate."

Becks smiles. "Hot chocolate sounds good."

Beck follows me to the guest house. Once inside, we head to the kitchen. Beck stands across from me, right next to the cabinet with the mugs in. I switch on the jug first before reaching up to grab two mugs. Beck reaches up as I do, grabbing one while I grab the other. We set the mugs down on the counter and stand there staring at each other, our bodies completely aware of how close we are. I can feel the heat bouncing off Beck, and all I want is to be wrapped in it.

I think about the other day when we were here, how we almost went all the way but stopped because there was something stopping me. Now when I stand here in the kitchen with Beck, I know this time I could go all the way. I need to let go of Dean. He would want me to be happy and fall in love again.

"Beck, these last two years have been hard for me," I say. "Some days I don't know how to keep living without Dean. I hold on to him like he is still here with me, and sometimes I can feel him. But since you came here, I feel like my life has changed, like I have a reason to move on. I don't know if it's a coincidence or there is a reason you are here, but I'm happy you are here."

Beck smiles. "I'm glad I'm here too."

"You remind me of Dean in some ways."

Beck arches his eyebrow. "Yeah? In what way?"

"You are caring and protective. You listen to me when I need someone to talk to, even when I don't want to talk."

He stares at me with a serious look. "There's someone I know who I seriously hurt in the past, and I want to make sure I protect them." His hands find my waist and pull me towards him. "I want to protect you."

My stomach dances with butterflies.

"You don't need to protect me, Beck."

"But I need to," he says in a whisper.

"Why do you feel you need to?"

He lifts his hand, stroking my cheek. "With what happened to you with Dean, I want to make sure you don't go through something like that again."

I smile at him. "I won't go through that again because I have you, Beck. You are the reason I'm able to move on."

I place a hand on his chest, looking up at him. He observes me. "Beck..." I breathe.

A voice in my head tells me to back away, that I will get myself hurt again if I let someone in. But there's the other half of me that is curious about what could happen if I step out of my comfort zone, exploring a relationship with Beck. Dean would want me to take this step.

We stare at each other for a long time. The jug stops boiling, but neither of us moves to switch it off.

Beck drew in a breath and then makes the first move. He cups his hands around my jaw and kisses me. I move my hand from his chest and wrap my arms around his neck, pulling myself closer to him. Beck slides his hands down my body until he reaches my waist and lifts me up onto the counter. His hands move to my thighs as he stands between my legs, and I wrap them around his waist.

Beck's lips move down to my neck. A soft moan escapes my lips as he bites down on the skin.

"Are you sure you want to do this, Emma?" Beck asks me, kissing up my neck to my jaw.

I nod, a gasp escaping my lips. "Yes, I do."

"I don't want you to feel pressure. You also said you wanted to move slow. Isn't this moving too fast?"

Am I moving too fast? Am I truly ready for this?

But then again, am I ever going to be ready to move on?

"I want this, Beck. I want to move on from the past, and I want to move on... with you."

Beck smiles and lifts me off the counter. He then moves us to my room and lays me gently on my bed.

Chapter 21

Beck

I should have said something. I should have told Emma the truth about everything, about who I am. But when I look at her, mesmerised by her beauty, I wonder how could I break someone like her? This time, Emma doesn't stop me. It's me who should stop her, but I don't. We go all the way.

And it's eating me alive to know what I did to her boyfriend. What kind of person am I for having sex with her when I know I killed her boyfriend? This is so wrong, yet being with Emma feels right.

I lie down next to her, and she cuddles up to me, our naked skin pressing up against each other. One of my hands is interlaced with hers while my other arm is wrapped around her. She is so beautiful. I just can't break her heart. Can I not tell her the truth?

I don't regret this moment with her. But I don't know how I can tell her the truth.

I'm falling for this woman, and I can't tell her my darkest secret. Telling her will mean I will lose her for good, and I don't want to.

"Do you ever wonder how someone can make you feel good after you thought you lost everything?" Emma asks, interrupting my thoughts.

I let go of her hand and rest mine on her jaw, gently stroking her skin with my thumb. I have never been in love, not until Emma. We haven't known each other for long, but I'm falling for her fast. The moment my world turned upside down, I didn't think anything would go back to normal. And then when Emma walked into my life, it was like everything had changed. When I came out of jail, I had no idea how everything was going to be. I knew I wasn't welcome around Middleton, that the whole town would hate me for what I did, their judging eyes following me everywhere. Here in Maisy Grove, no one knows me or what I've done. Annie isn't judgemental, and I'm grateful she has given me a chance. And I don't know if it's luck, but I am glad Emma doesn't know who I am, that she was not at the court cases. It won't be long until she knows the truth. Despite keeping the secret from her, she makes me feel good whenever I am around her.

Which I knew once the truth will be expose, nothing was going to end well.

"I wonder that all the time," I answer. "When I came out of jail, I wondered if I would ever be happy again. And then I met you, and my world changed. You make me happy, Emma."

She smiles at me. "You make me happy too, Beck."

I return a smile, unsure if it's real. How can I fall in love with someone despite knowing I've hurt her? I'm the cause of her pain, and she'll hate me forever when she finds out.

I lean in and kiss her softly, cupping my hand around her jaw as I use the arm to pull her closer to me. I don't want to be reminded of my past. I want to forget it all and be with Emma.

I pull back and stare into her blue eyes as she stares back at me. She's so beautiful. I can't break her heart.

"I love you, Emma," my voice a loud whisper.

"I love you too," she returns.

"Do you think we should go back to the kitchen and make that hot chocolate and then maybe check on Annie in case she comes looking for us?"

Emma laughs, the sound of it making my stomach do a somersault. "I'm sure she isn't going to come looking for us. She'll probably think we're somewhere around the farm. And yes, I'll go and make you one."

Emma pecks my lips and then climbs out of bed, picking up her clothing off the floor.

Why am I so stupid? How long can I keep this secret from Emma?

I need to get out of here. I need to go somewhere to think.

I call up Chandler. He answers on the fifth ring. "Hey, are you busy?"

"I'm cooking dinner with Lisa. What's up, mate?"

"I need to get out of here and think. Can you come get me?"

I hear what sounds like Chandler grabbing his keys. "Sure. Is everything alright, Beck?"

Tears prick at my eyelids when he asks me. No. I'm not alright. I should be feeling on top of the world right now, but I would be lying if I said I was alright. Everything about today with Dad and then Emma, I'm not sure how much more I can take with lying to her. I don't know how I'll be able to take the rejection once she finds out the truth. And no doubt I can't stay at the farm. Where was I going to go? The last thing I wanted was to come back to

Middleton and bump into my dad. I don't want to see that jerk for as long as I live.

"No," I answer. "Nothing is alright."

My head is spinning with so many thoughts that I don't even know what I should actually think about. In the past, when I'm feeling like this, especially when I'm around Dad and he makes me feel like crap, the first thing I do is grab beer or whatever the closest alcoholic beverage is to me. For that small moment of time, alcohol eases the thoughts in my head and calms me, putting an end to the spiralling.

At first, without choice, I'm now sober for over two years. Now, all I can think about is opening up a can of beer, anything to make me forget what I'm keeping from Emma. Of course I know it isn't going to solve anything, because every time I look at her, I think about the past. I just can't stand to think about it. Would it be bad if I just had one beer? I can stop at one beer.

Maybe if I have one beer or two, it will help me erase the words dad told me earlier at the pub, how he makes me wish I was dead. And maybe for a moment it will help me forget about Dean, how I took away an innocent life. All because I was selfish as I drank one glass after another until I couldn't walk. Can I forget the night ever happened?

I let Annie know that I'm seeing a friend and am not sure when I'll be back for dinner. I then leave the house before Emma sees me and asks questions. I can't look at her. Not right now. Not without thinking about what a selfish jerk I am for sleeping with her after I accidentally killed her boyfriend.

Instead of waiting at the end of the driveway for Chandler, I decide to make my own way into town. Who knows how long I'll be waiting on him, and maybe a good walk would help me clear my mind. There's a pub in town. Maybe I can meet Chandler there instead. So, I text him to let him know where to meet.

My feet are killing me by the time I get to the local pub. The walk into town is at least thirty minutes, maybe more. I stand outside for a long time, staring at the menu, hesitating about going in and ordering a beer. One should be enough. I don't have to drink any more than that. I won't hurt anyone or myself if I have just one beer.

I enter the pub and walk over to the counter, ordering a beer. I watch the bartender pour it into a glass. I pay for it and then sit down at a table. I don't drink it at first, instead I stare at it in front of me. At the back of my mind, I know what I'm doing is wrong, but then there's the other half of me that says just one couldn't hurt. I remember the taste of the cold beer Dad had forced me to drink earlier. There should be no harm in having another drink.

I hold the glass in my hand and gulp half of the drink down when Chandler walks in. His eyes lock with mine from across the room, and I immediately feel the guilt sweeping in. How could I even begin to think that this is a great idea to start drinking again? Who am I kidding, that I would keep this as one drink? Why would I even want to start drinking after everything that happened? The last thing I want is to do something stupid and end up in jail again.

Chandler races across the room to me, grabbing the glass, but I can't let him take it.

"What are you doing, Beck?" he asks me. "Don't you remember what happened the last time you drank?"

Of course I do. It's the day that follows me with every breath.

"Why does it matter, anyway?" I say. "I'm worthless."

"You aren't worthless, Beck. Let go of the glass. I'll get you a Coke."

I shake my head. "I don't want a Coke."

I try to move the glass towards me, but Chandler pulls it towards him

"Beck, listen to me. I'm not going to let you fall into this habit again. How many have you had already?"

"My dad forced me to have one earlier. And now I've done something so stupid that the only thing I can do is drink like I always do."

Chandler curses. "You saw your dad?"

I nod. "I shouldn't have gone to see him, but he threatened me if I didn't come."

"Okay, well, let go of the glass, Beck. I'll get us a Coke, and then you can tell me everything."

I don't let go of the glass. I try to fight for it, but it's no use. Chandler is dead set on telling me to let go. And I don't want to cause a scene over a half glass of beer. So I surrender. As soon as I do, Chandler moves it out of my reach and then hugs me.

"It's okay, mate," he tells me. "Everything is alright."

Chandler lets me go and then takes the glass to the counter while I wait for him at the table. I sit there, lost in my thoughts, until Chandler returns, setting our new, non-alcoholic drinks down. I grab the glass and take a sip, thanking Chandler. He waits a few minutes before asking me to tell him everything.

So I tell him about Dad and what he made me do. And then I tell him about Emma.

Chandler stares at me for a moment, processing everything. He doesn't ask me about Dad but he does ask me about Emma. "You haven't told Emma what you did?"

I shake my head, not daring to look at him. "No, I haven't."

Chandler sighs. "Beck, you should have told her before you decided to sleep with her."

I force myself to look at him. "I know, Chandler. I've tried to tell her, but I can't find the right words. I can't find it in me to break her heart. I'm falling for her. I can't tell her the truth."

"There are never going to be the right words to tell her. And the longer you don't tell her, the more upset she's going to be. Also, sleeping with her just made it worse."

I hate how Chandler is right. I've made it worse between us.

"She's going to hate me. I don't know how I can deal with that. It will also mean that I need to move and change jobs because surely she's not going to want me there. I don't want to leave. Annie is the only person who has given me a chance. I won't get another chance once I leave."

Chandler nods. "I understand, Beck. But sometimes these things happen. Whatever happens, I'll support you. For now, you need to tell her the truth."

I know I need to, but still, I have no idea how to tell her. The truth is too hard to admit.

"Beck," Chandler says. "Promise me you won't go back to drinking. I don't want you to end up a mess again."

I stare at the glass of Coke in front of me before answering. "I promise."

"And promise me you'll tell Emma everything."

That I can't promise him, but I have to do it.

Chapter 22

Beck

Days turn into weeks, and before I know it, it's a month. Each day I don't tell Emma the truth; it eats me up inside. I'm a dick for not telling her.

There are so many times when I could have told her. Like when we are fooling around in bed, or when we sneak kisses in between my shift, or when we take trips down to the river. With the help of Emma, Buckley has been warming up to me. Yet, not once could I let it slip that I'm the reason Dean is no longer here. I know what will happen once I tell her, and I dread the thought. I will lose Emma, and then I will lose this job that I have come to enjoy. There was still so much money I needed to save to move to a place here in Maisy Grove, where my mother will live with me, and be safe.

As much as I promise myself and Chandler I wasn't going to drink, I did get myself drunk one night. I brought myself a bottle of whisky, sat in my room and curse at myself for being a coward for not telling the Emma the truth. Then I cried myself to sleep, hating myself for letting dad get to me, for drowning my fear with alcohol, just like I have always done in the past. Especially the night when I killed Dean.

You're an idiot, Beck. Why won't you tell her anything? Why did you get behind the wheel that night?

I need to tell Emma. Why was it hard to find the right words and tell her everything?

Now, as I stand in front of the mirror in my room, getting ready for Emma's brother's wedding, I knew my luck for keeping this secret was running out fast. What are the odds that no one at the wedding will recognise me? I thought of pretending to be sick, but I can't back out of this. Even if I skip out on this event, there will be other family gatherings where Emma will use me to go to. I can't keep this secret forever. Eventually all secrets are exposed.

"Everything will be fine, Beck," I tell my reflection as I do up my tie.

But I know deep inside, nothing was going to be okay.

Emma is going to hate me after today. This wedding is going to be a disaster.

Chapter 23

Emma

"Are you nervous about meeting my family?" I ask Beck as I drive us to the venue of the wedding ceremony. Kristy and Daniel chose the Callington's Estate for their wedding venue here in Maisy Grove, which has the most spectacular view overlooking the vineyard. I can't believe how fast the three weeks has gone, and how my brother was finally getting married.

Beck doesn't answer straight away, he simply nods. "Yeah, pretty much."

I turn to look at him briefly before turning my eyes back to the road. Beck looks so handsome in his black suit and blue tie to match my dress. He hasn't shaved, and has a stubble growing.

"Don't be nervous," I tell him. "My family is going to love you."

"I don't know," he answers. "Many people judge me after finding out I've gone to jail."

"I promise you my family will not judge you."

Sure, my parents will be uncomfortable at first hearing that I've met a guy who has gotten out of jail. Though it isn't like he's a serial killer or someone really dangerous. The only person I'm worried about the most is Daniel. Being overprotective, I know he isn't going to like Beck as much as I want him to. I understand. He doesn't want to see me get hurt again, but still, I don't want him threatening my boyfriend. Beck isn't going to hurt me.

It's fairly early when we arrive. So far, it's only Kristy and her friends are here, getting themselves ready for the big day. None of the guests or my brother are here yet. I leave my car keys with Beck, telling him he can sit in the car for a bit before everyone arrives. He agrees to, and I get out to meet with Kristy.

For the next few hours, Kristy's friends and I get ready together. She looked stunning in her dress, with her hair in a side braid with flowers. The bridesmaid and I do a loose bun for our hair. Soon enough, it's time to walk Kristy outside to the altar. The ceremony is outside, with the vineyard as the backdrop. Later, we'll be moving inside the venue for the reception.

Kristy and Daniel don't have a ring bearer or flower girl, so Tracey is the first to walk down the aisle, followed by Sandra. I follow close behind Sandra. As I walk, I look around to see where Beck is. I spot him straight away, sitting in the back row. As soon as our eyes meet, his eyes widen at the sight of me. I smile at him, and then continue following Tracey and Sandra until we reach the end of the aisle. My parents sit in the front row behind my brother and his groomsmen. Daniel turns to look down the aisle as Kristy begins to walk down, tears in his eyes.

The ceremony goes smoothly as Kristy and Daniel exchange their vows, and they are now married.

Once the ceremony is over, we gather in the back, talking with friends and family and congratulating the newlyweds as we pose for photos. We wait for the venue staff to tell us when they are ready for everyone to move into the reception.

I walk over to Beck, greeting him with a kiss.

"You look beautiful, Emma," he says.

I smile. "Thanks, Beck."

"Emma!"

I turn to the voice behind me, and see my friends Sammy and Katie walking over to me. Their matching brunette hair hangs loose around their shoulders in curls. Neither of them smiles as they look between Beck and me.

"Guys, hey," I greet them with a hug. "It's so good to see you. I want you to meet someone. Katie, Sammy, this is my boyfriend, Beck. Beck, these are my friends Katie and Sammy."

I expect my friends to be all smiles when they see Beck, happy that I've met someone after Dean's death at the very least. But they just stand there, staring at him like he's some stranger they shouldn't be talking to. They don't even say hi to him.

"Is everything okay?" I ask them.

"Emma, can we talk to you for a second?" Katie asks.

I look between Katie and Sammy. What could they possibly want to talk about right now? I turn to Beck and tell him I won't be long.

My friends and I move aside, moving to the middle of the aisle.

"What's wrong?" I ask them.

Katie looks over my shoulder and then back to me. "What are you doing with Beck, Emma? How is that guy your boyfriend?"

"He can't be your boyfriend," Sammy adds before I get a chance to answer. "Do you have any idea who Beck is?"

I stare at my friends with a puzzled look. What on earth are they talking about? "I thought you guys would be happy I'm seeing someone. Why are you acting like this?"

Sammy and Katie exchange looks, like they're having a silent conversation about who should be telling me whatever news I probably don't want to hear.

"That man cannot be your boyfriend," Katie says.

"You can't be with him because he's Beckett Owens," Sammy adds.

I stare at my friends, unsure if I'm supposed to recognise this name. Beck has never told me his full name. Am I supposed to know his full name?

"What are you guys on about?" I ask.

"Emma, this is why you should have paid attention to the court stuff," Katie tells me. "That way, you can avoid this man."

"Beckett Owens is the one who crashed into you and killed Dean," Sammy bursts out.

I freeze at what she said, looking between them, wondering, hoping that this is some kind of joke.

But I'm dead wrong.

I turn around to face Beck. Our eyes meet, locked in each other's stares. How could this man I have fallen in love with be the person who killed my boyfriend? And then it makes sense. Beck was extremely nervous about attending the wedding because he knew he would be recognised. This is it. This is his secret that he couldn't tell me. It has been a month, and not once did he not tell me the truth.

A knot appeared in my stomach, making me nauseous. How could I be so stupid to fall for someone and not know they are the one who is responsible for killing my boyfriend?

I take my time slowly, walking over to him, our eyes never leaving each other. I have never given any thought to what I would actually do if I ever came across the man who crashed into us. Now he is standing in front of me, and all I feel is disgust.

Beck continues to stare back at me, waiting for me to say something. He knows I now know. There's no hiding it anymore.

"Is it true, Beck?" I ask. "Are you Beckett Owens? The person who crashed into Dean and me?"

Beck opens his mouth to speak but closes it. He doesn't need to say anything or confess everything because him being speechless is enough for me to know that what my friends have told me is true.

"Why didn't you tell me, Beck?" I ask him. "We have been together for a month! How did Annie even allow you to work on the farm? Does Annie know who you are?"

He shakes his head. "No, Annie doesn't know. Emma, I'm sorry."

I frown. Does he really think I'm going to accept his apology? "Don't you dare say you're sorry, because you aren't."

"Let me explain, Emma."

"No. What is there to explain? You killed Dean!"

Someone curses behind me. Before I can turn to see who it is, I'm pushed out of the way. Daniel now stands in front of me, his fist at his side.

"You have a lot of nerve showing up here," he says.

"Your sister invited me," Beck points out.

"Yeah? Well, I'm uninviting you."

Without another word, Daniel swings his fist, knocking Beck in the jaw. Beck steps back from the blow, and Kristy runs over to them. A crowd starts forming around us.

"Daniel, no!" Kristy cries. "Not here."

Daniel turns to his wife and points to Beck. "How could you approve him on the guest list?"

Kristy looks at him, innocently. "I didn't know."

Daniel turns back to Beck and shoves him hard in the chest. "You stay away from my sister! You can also stay away from the rest of my family. Now leave, or I'll call the cops on you for crashing my wedding."

Beck's eyes widen, filling with fear. "No, please. Don't call the police."

My brother shoves him again. "Then get out of here!"

Dad comes up behind him and places his hands on my brother's shoulders. "That's enough, Daniel." He then looks at Beck. "You heard my son. Get out of here."

Beck takes a step forward, only looking at me. I shake my head at him, then turn and run towards the car park.

"Emma!" Beck calls out.

I stop for a moment, taking off my heels to run better. I'm not about to break my neck here while running from the man who killed my boyfriend.

"Emma, wait!"

I reach the car park, but before I can escape into my car, Beck is behind me and grabs my arm. I stop, turn around and lash out at him, shoving Beck hard in the chest with my free arm.

"Let go of me!" I scream.

To my surprise, Beck listens and drops his hand. "Emma, I'm very sorry. Let me explain."

"Explain what, Beck? How you've tricked me into falling for you while you're secretly the person I never want to see again after what happened to Dean?"

"I didn't trick you, Emma. I didn't know who you were at first until you told me about Dean. I know I should have told you then who I was, but I was afraid to tell you. We were getting along well, and I was beginning to fall for you. I didn't want you to think of me as the person who killed your boyfriend. I wanted you to like me for who I am now. I'm not the person I was two years ago."

I shake my head. How does he think I could ever like him for the person he is now? Maybe he isn't the person he was two years ago, but still, I can't be with the person who killed my boyfriend.

"You know, after Dean died, I refrained from watching the news reports anything to do with the courts because I didn't want to be reminded of what happened," I explain. "I didn't even want to know the name of the driver who hit us. I figured, what was the point in knowing who the person was when I was never going to come across them again. But now, I wonder if I should have listened to the reports, that way I would have known who you were as soon as I saw you on the farm."

"And what would you have done if you had known who I was?"

I stare at him, thinking quickly. What would I have said to him? "I don't know. But I would have told Annie to fire you before you even began work. And right now, I'm going to go back home, and I'm going to tell Annie everything. I never want to see you again."

Fears flashes in Beck's eyes. "Emma, no. Listen to me. I need this job. Annie is the only person who was willing to take me in because of my criminal record."

"It's not my problem, Beck. Or should I call you Beckett?"

He winces as if my words were a slap to his face.

"I can't have you working on the farm while I'm there. I can't be around the person who killed my boyfriend and almost killed me too," I say.

I turn to walk to the car but Beck reaches for me again. As soon as his hand touches me, I swing around, shoving him. He begs me to listen, but how can I listen to him?

"Let go of me!" I scream.

Friends and family start crowding around the car. I see my dad and brother leading the way. Daniel looking like he might kill Beck.

"You can't expect me to forgive you," I tell Beck. "What you did, you took the most important person away from me. And I can't be around someone like you." I nod towards the forming crowd. "Now, you better get out of here before my brother comes over here. He isn't kidding about calling the cops on you. And I don't care how you get home, but you aren't coming with me."

"Emma, don't leave me stranded here."

"I am. I don't want you anywhere near me. And when you get back to the farm, start packing your bags because I'll make sure Annie throws you out."

"Emma, please don't do this. Please don't hate me. I know I can't change what happened, but I'll do whatever I can to make it up to you."

"You can't make it up to me, Beck. You took away the person I love more than anything in this world. How do you expect me to ever forgive you or not to hate you?" I shake my head, the tears filling my eyes, but I force myself to hold them. I'm not going to burst into tears right here in front of Beck. "I'm sorry, but I just can't be around you." I hold out my hand. "Give me my keys."

Beck grabs my keys from his pocket and then places them in my hand. Without another word, I get over to my car and jump in, quickly locking the doors so Beck doesn't jump in. He runs to the car, banging on the window, begging me to let him in, but I ignore him. Instead, I turn the ignition and shift the gear into drive, slowly moving out of the space. But he's still there, running alongside the moving car, still begging me to open the door. When it was safe to do so, I put my foot down on the accelerator, leaving Beck behind. I don't even look through the review mirror.

Chapter 24

Emma

I wait until I'm a few metres from the vineyard before pulling over. As soon as I do, I cover my face with my hands and cry. It comes out as loud sobs. How could I have been so damn stupid for falling for Beck? How did I not know he was the drunk driver who ran into us?

If I had just followed the trail, I would have known his name. And as soon as I saw him the first day he had arrived at the farm, I would have been able to identify him, and I would have told Annie to fire him. It's no wonder he refused to tell me his secret because he knew how I would react when I found out. And the fact he kept it a secret from me for a whole month! How could he do this to me?

For a moment I was expecting my phone to ring, and either my parents, brother or Kristy would be calling to make sure I am okay. But then I remember I left my phone in the dressing room. I can't go back for it. I can't face everyone there, especially not Beck.

When I calm down and have wiped my eyes, I start the car again. At first, I think of going home, but then I think of the one place I haven't been to for a while.

So I head towards Middleton, to the cemetery where Dean was laid to rest.

I walk barefoot through the cemetery until I come to Dean's grave, kneeling on the grass in front of his tombstone and weep.

"I'm sorry, Dean," I say. "I'm so sorry. I didn't know Beck was the driver. I feel so stupid, Dean. I shouldn't have fallen for him. It was a mistake. I thought I could move on, but not with him."

I stare at his tombstone, waiting for an answer that was never coming. I reach out and run my fingers along the engraved letters of his name.

"I miss you every day, Dean. I wish you were here with me."

The tears come out fast again, and I have no control over them. I just let them fall. I don't remember the last time I've cried this much over Dean. But right now, the thought of moving on and leaving Dean in the past feels like a mistake. For the past two years, I've kept my distance from everyone, shutting myself out over the accident. And then the moment I allow someone in, someone who I thought cared, he ends up being the person who crashed into us. If Beck hadn't gotten behind the wheel that night, Dean would still be here.

I don't stay at the cemetery for long. I figure someone is bound to know to look for me here, and right now, I don't want to talk to my family or my friends about what happened. It'll only make me feel more like a fool for not recognising my own boyfriend's killer. Of all the times they tried to tell me who he was, I cut them off, not wanting to know the name of the person. Beckett Owens.

The last person I want to find me here is Beck. I don't think he'll look for me here, but he could. Honestly, I just hope he's back at the farm, packing his things and leaving. He'd better be gone by the time I get home.

The clouds were growing darker in the distance. The forecast said there was going to be a thunderstorm later this afternoon. It was best to head home before I get caught in the storm.

Annie comes out of the house once I arrive home with Jessie at her heels. Jessie runs over to me, barking happily. I kneel down to pat her. Thunder rumbles quietly in the distance. The storm is getting closer now. It won't be long before it's here.

"Emma, you're home early," she says, looking towards the car and then back to me, probably eyeing my smudged mascara. "Is everything alright? Where's Beck?"

"I don't know, and I don't care. Did you know he was the one who caused the accident and killed my boyfriend, Annie?"

Annie's mouth hangs slightly open. I expect her to tell me that she already knows, but from the look of her, I guess Beck was telling the truth. Annie didn't know the truth about him.

"No, I didn't know." She comes down the stairs towards me. "Emma, I'm so sorry."

I step back. I can't be here right now. Not when Beck could come back soon. "I'm going to take Blondie for a ride."

Annie presses her lips together. Jessie walks back over to Annie and sits down beside her feet. "Emma, come on inside. I can make us some tea, and we can chat if you want."

"Maybe later, Annie. I need to clear my head."

"Emma, I don't think it's a good idea to take Blondie for a ride. There's a storm coming, and you know the horses don't like the sound of thunder."

"I'll be back before the storm hits."

Or maybe I won't be back until Beck is packed up and gone.

I head into the barn and grab Blondie's riding gear. When I reach her, she's unsettled, probably hearing the thunder in the distance. The other horses also seem a little unsettled.

"Hey, Blondie," I say to her, rubbing her snout. "It's okay. Let's go for a ride."

Blondie calms down from my touch, and I start putting on the saddle and the reins.

The clouds are growing darker as they move closer to our town, but the thunder still seems far. Blondie and I head to the river, which is probably not the wisest thing to do, but where else can I go without running into Beck? I don't care how he got back here. I just don't want to ever see him again.

At the river, I let Blondie gaze on the grass while I sit by, watching the water, lost in my own thoughts. I think of all the times I've been down here with Beck. I want to believe we had something between us, and maybe we did, but Beck and I can never be together. I just can't be with someone who claimed my boyfriend's life and almost took mine. Maybe he has changed since going to jail, but that doesn't change what he has done.

All of the times he hesitated when I questioned him, I should have known. And there's some of the conversation I heard with his dad and him, talking about someone he had killed. I didn't think it would be Dean. How could I have been so oblivious?

But then I remember why I fell for him. He reminded me of Dean. He was caring and loving. I can't forget the day where he was willing to go up to Darcy and Roxanne to defend me, even when I told him not to. I think of the way his lips felt against mine, reminding of what it felt to be in love. He was helping me to move on from Dean.

A loud clap of thunder suddenly rumbles in the sky, making me jump and startling Blondie. We need to go.

I get up and try to calm my horse down. Blondie watches me carefully as I rub her snout before climbing onto her. Just as I'm about to grab the rein with my other hand, another clap of thunder rumbles, startling Blondie, causing her to buckle, throwing me off. I hit the ground.

Chapter 25

Beck

I'm stranded.

There's no way for me to get back home. Out here in the country, there isn't much transport to take, and I don't have the money to catch an Uber.

I glance behind me to see Emma's dad and brother have stopped following me, and I sigh with relief. I shouldn't have come today. What was I thinking? Of course someone would recognise me and spill the beans to Emma before I even had the chance to. But then again, was I ever going to tell her the truth?

What's going to happen when she tells Annie everything? Would Annie listen to her and fire me? I honestly don't know what I'll do if Annie kicks me out. The only place I can go is back to Chandler and Lisa's place. But if I move back to Middleton, I'll surely bump into Dad there. I can just imagine all the things he'd say to me now.

I pull out my phone, knowing that the only person who could help me right now is Chandler. So I wait on the side of the road until he arrives, when he asks me to explain everything

"I blew it, man," I answer. "I mean, I know I should have confessed to her about everything, but I didn't know how to because I didn't want to ruin anything between us. I just didn't want to lose her. Her friends recognised me, told her, and now her brother wants to kill me. Emma took off and told me she's going to tell Annie everything and make her fire me."

"Well, let her calm down, and then maybe the two of you can talk it out. Do you have any idea where she could be?"

I think for a moment. I have no clue where she could be.

"Let's just go home," I answer. "Maybe that's where she'll be."

Chandler heads in the direction of Annie's farm.

I spot Emma's car the moment Chandler pulls up at the house, and I jump out before Chandler has the chance to put on the brakes. There's no one inside the car, so I run towards her guest house. Thunder roars in the distance.

I bang on the front door.

"Emma, open the door, please!" I call out. "Let me explain everything."

No response. I try to look through the windows, but she has the blinds closed.

Perhaps she isn't in the guest house but inside the main house. That's probably where she would go, wouldn't it? She's close to Annie, so I assume she's probably with her, talking to her about everything.

I walk around to the front where I hear Jessie barking. I see the dog with Annie, where she stands outside her home, talking with Chandler. I jog back over to them.

"Annie, where's Emma?" I ask. "I really need to talk to her."

A big fat raindrop falls on top of my head. I look up at the clouds above me as the rain comes down pouring. We move under the veranda.

"Emma took off on Blondie," Annie explains. "I told her not to take her out because of the storm, but she didn't listen. I've been keeping an eye out for her, but she hasn't returned yet."

Behind us, a horse neighs in panic. We turn to see Blondie running across the field, running towards the barn, running without Emma on her back.

I curse, wondering what could have happened. It's all my fault she's out there.

The three of us run out into the rain, heading over to the horse who calms down when she sees Annie. Annie takes the reins, stroking the horse's snout, telling her everything is okay.

"Where's Emma?" I question. "There is no way she wouldn't let Blondie run off like that."

"My guess is that Blondie got spooked by the thunder and took off, leaving Emma behind," Annie says. "I'm going to take Blondie back to the barn and calm her down, maybe check on the other horses as well. Are you boys able to go look for her and make sure she's okay?"

I nod. "Will do, Annie."

I lead the way in the direction Blondie came from. It rains down hard, making it difficult to see.

"Where do you think she is?" Chandler asks me.

There's only one place I could think Emma would be, and it's the river. She loved if there. So we make our way, Chandler following close behind me.

As soon as we get to the river, I spot Emma immediately, lifeless and on the ground. My heart drops to my stomach. She can't be dead. I run to her side, rolling her onto her back. There's a gash on her forehead where she must have hit it.

I tap her face gently. "Emma, can you hear me?"

"What happened to her?" Chandler asks as he kneels down beside me.

I shake my head. "I don't know. She could have tripped. Or maybe she fell off the horse."

"Is she alive?"

I place two fingers on her neck and feel a light pulse. I sigh with relief. She's alive.

I shake her gently. "Emma, wake up. Can you hear me? It's Beck."

Emma makes no movement.

"We need to get her back," I say, carefully lifting Emma into a sitting position. "Chandler, can you call for an ambulance?"

Chandler helps me get Emma off the ground, and I carefully carry her back to the farm, bridal style. Chandler calls for the ambulance.

When we get back, the ambulance hasn't arrived yet. But her parents are there, talking with Annie.

"Annie!" I yell out to her. "Help me, please!"

Annie gasps, running over to me. "What happened?"

"I don't know. I think she might have fallen off the horse. She isn't responding."

"The ambulance is on their way," Chandler says.

Emma's dad takes her from me. "What did you do to my daughter?"

"Nothing," I answer. "I swear. She was lying on the ground by the river when I found her."

Emma's mum gently strokes her cheek. "Emma, sweetie. Can you hear me?"

Sirens wail in the distance, and within seconds, the ambulance is parked nearby. The paramedics rush over with their stretcher to check Emma and start asking questions. I do my best to answer all of them. They shine a light in her eyes before saying which hospital they are taking her to.

Emma's dad turns to me, narrowing his eyes. He takes a step forward, towering over me. "You stay away from my daughter, you hear me? You have caused enough trouble for her."

"I'm sorry. For everything."

He shakes his head. "You aren't sorry. If I catch you anywhere near Emma, don't think I won't knock you out."

"George, enough." Emma's mum put her hand on her husband's arm.

Her dad stares at me with his dark eyes before turning away, heading towards his car.

Emma's mum promises Annie she will call her later to let her know how she is before getting in the car with her husband. They follow the ambulance down the gravel driveway, and all I can do is watch her leave. My vision is blurred from the heavy rain as I watch the lights of the ambulance drive away.

"Chandler, can you drive me to the hospital?"

Annie grabs my arm before I get the chance to get in his car.

"Beck, no." She turns me to face her. "Listen to me. You can't be at the hospital right now."

"Why not? I have to make sure she's okay."

"I know, and you can see her later. But right now, let this time just be for her family. You won't be able to see her. You can come with me later when she's allowed to have visitors other than family. Emma told me what happened. And from what I can see, I'm guessing her family knows who you are, and I don't think they are going to allow you to go near her."

I stare at Annie, a thousand things running through my head. I wait for Annie to say the words now that she knows, that I'm no longer welcome here, but she never says anything. And she's right. As much as I want to see Emma and be at the hospital with her, the nurses aren't going to allow me in unless I'm family. And if I enter the room, I'm sure Emma's dad or her brother will make sure I get arrested for coming near her. I can't get arrested again.

"Why don't you boys come on in out of the rain?" Annie suggests. "I've made some fresh iced tea."

Before I can answer her, my phone rings. Mum's name flashes across the screen.

"Hey, Mum."

"Beck, sweetie, help me, please." My body goes cold from the sound of Mum's voice. She sounds like she has been crying.

And it can only mean one thing.

"Did he hurt you? Where are you, Mum?"

I hear banging on the other side of the phone and yelling.

"I'm in the bathroom. Help me, Beck. Please."

"Hold on. I'm on my way."

I hang up and then run to Chandler's car. "Chandler, we need to go!"

Chapter 26

Beck

As soon as the car is put in brake, I get out and sprint across the lawn.

"Beck, wait!" Chandler calls after me. "What is the plan?"

I reach the steps of our veranda and turn to him. "We're going to go in there and get my mother out."

Chandler catches up to me and shakes his head. "No, we need a plan, Beck. We can't just barge in without a plan. What if your father has a knife or something? He probably knows your mother called you, or maybe this is just a set-up for you to come in."

Chandler's right. We can't just barge in without a plan. The truth is, I don't know what kind of plan to go with. But what I do know is Dad is here, so I know he hasn't left the house.

Quietly, I walk onto the veranda and peek through the window. There's no movement inside. I silently pray that Mum is still safe inside the bathroom and Dad hasn't managed to do something. What if we don't have any time to make a plan?

"Why don't you stay out here and call the police?" I suggest. "Tell them there's a domestic dispute."

Chandler looks through the window and then back at me. "Are you sure? What if you need help?"

"I'm going to need help. That's why I said to call for the police, because there is no way the two of us can take my dad on our own."

I may never have called the police in the past, but this time I needed to protect my mother. This has gone on for so long that it's about time it stopped. I need Mum to be safe, and neither of us will be safe until he's arrested and put in jail where he belongs.

Chandler makes the call.

Meanwhile, I open the door slowly. The house is quiet, and I don't see my dad anywhere. I stand at the front door for a moment, listening for any movement. There are empty beer bottles on the coffee table in the lounge room. Dad could be anywhere in the house, and I have no idea what he will do to me if he sees me here.

I creep through the house to the bathroom. The door is closed, and I knock softly.

"Mum?" I call. "Mum, it's me, Beck."

I hear her fiddling with the lock before opening the door. She stands there, her eyes red and puffy. There are new bruises on her face, and I wonder if it is from today or another day. She is also cradling her left arm that looks like it could be dislocated. I curse softly, hating myself for not being here for my mother.

Mum tries to smile but it doesn't quite reach her eyes.

I rest my hand on the back of my mother's back and push her slowly along. "Come on, Mum. Let's get you out of here."

But before I can take a step, a hand grabs my arm, pulling me away from my mother. Mum cries out, and then a fist knocks me in the jaw. I hit my head on the back of the door frame. I try to gain my balance, but I fall to the floor. I look up, and there's Dad, looking down at me with an evil smile curled on his lips. There's an angry look in his eyes, telling me I can't trust him. Hopefully

Chandler has managed to get a hold of the police, and they will be here any minute.

"You always have to be a hero, don't you, Beck?" Dad says.

Mum pushes in front of Dad. "Stanley, stop. Don't do this."

Dad pushes Mum aside, and she is thrown to the floor. She cries out in pain as she lands on the arm she has been cradling. Dad starts spitting insults at her, telling her to stay out of this.

I stand up. "Stop speaking to her like that, Dad. Enough is enough."

He turns, his brown eyes narrowing at me and his nostrils flaring. "Don't ever tell me what I should be doing."

Dad throws another punch, but this time, I'm prepared, and I managed to block it. He then knees me hard in the crotch, and I yelp. Dad then pushes me to the floor and kicks me hard in the stomach. I gasp for breath from the blow, hardly able to focus on my breathing when he aims his foot at me again.

"Leave him alone!" I hear Chandler's voice come from the doorway.

I look over at my best friend and watch him jump behind my dad and wrap his arms around his neck. Dad shakes him off and knocks him to the floor.

"Chandler," I groan as I sit up. "Get my mother out of here."

Dad strolls over to me, his fists clenched. I stand up, and he tries to take another swing at me, but I manage to dodge him. Out of the corner of my eye, I see Chandler helping my mother get to her feet, and together, they make a run for the front door. I wonder if I could make a run for it too.

"Dad, don't do this," I tell him. "Just calm down."

Dad grabs me by the shoulders and slams me against the wall. A picture frame falls, and the glass shatters on impact. "Don't you tell me what to do."

He slams me against the wall again and I hit the back of my head. I try to push my dad off, but he is so much stronger than me. I wish the police would just get here already and take him away. I think of how my mother and I will finally be safe from him after all of these years.

And then, in the distance, I hear the sirens. The police will be here soon.

Dad narrows his eyes. "You think you can be a hero by calling the police?"

I don't tell him it was Chandler who called them. "It's the only way I know Mum and I will be safe from you."

Dad laughs. "You think you can be safe from me? I'll make sure you aren't. You can throw me in jail, but I will find you, and I will make sure I will make your life hell. Don't try to be a hero, Beck. You'll always be a coward. Look what you did to that young man when you smashed into him. You were a coward for drinking your sorrows away instead of facing your fear with me."

I frown at him. That may be so, but I'm stronger than I was two years ago. I'm not afraid of my father anymore.

The sirens get closer.

"No, Dad," I say. "You're the one who is a coward."

Dad's eyes narrow, his whole face turning into a person I don't recognise. What's he going to do to me now? Will he kill me?

He lets go and moves away from me. I rub the back of my throbbing head and watch as he smashes one of his beer bottles on the coffee table, pointing the sharded glass directly at me. The police pull up outside, and I hope they get in here before Dad does anything.

I should run, but I stand there, frozen in fear of what Dad is going to do. He's going to kill me.

And if he does kill me, maybe it will be a good thing. I should have died in the accident instead of Dean. Dean didn't deserve what I did to him. Emma doesn't deserve to have someone like me.

Dad raises the glass. "Don't ever speak that way to me again!"

Before I have the chance to move away, Dad strikes me across my left cheek. I scream.

"Freeze!"

"Put your weapon down!"

Dad makes eye contact with me as he drops the broken glass bottle, shattering to pieces. The police officers walk behind him.

"This isn't over, Beck," Dad says.

One officer puts Dad's hands behind his back and handcuffs him. The other officer approaches me.

"Are you alright, sir?"

I nod, touching the side of my bloody cheek. I look over at Dad as he is escorted out of the house. He is swearing and saying all kinds of insults to the police, and when he sees Chandler and Mum out there, he starts spitting out insults to them.

"Let's get you cleaned up," the officer next to me says. "We'll get the paramedics to check you out." He then speaks into his radio, requesting an ambulance to this address.

We go outside, where I see Chandler and Mum standing on the front lawn. As soon as they see me, their faces light up with relief.

As I watch Dad get put in the back of the patrol car, I can let out a sigh with relief. After being abused for all of my life, my mother and I were finally free from it all.

Chapter 27

Emma

Mum and Dad are sitting beside me when I wake up. I look at them with a puzzled look, wondering what they are doing here when they should be at Daniel and Kristy's wedding. And then, when I look around, I realise I'm not in my room, but in the hospital. Then I feel it. The pounding in the back of my head.

I groan at the pain. My parents leap off their chairs and are immediately at my side.

Mum takes my hand and squeezes it, smiling. "Hey, honey. It's good to see you are awake."

"What happened?" I ask. "Why am I in the hospital? And why aren't you at the wedding?" I look past my parents, expecting Daniel and Kristy to walk in. "Where's Daniel and Kristy?"

"They're still at their wedding. We didn't want to inform them what had happened."

"Beckett Owens found you lying on the river bed," Dad tells me. His tone of voice sounds weird like he hates the idea of saying Beck's name.

At the thought of the river, everything comes back to me. Riding Blondie to the river, even when Annie told me not to. With the storm approaching fast, being beside the river and under the trees was dangerous. Blondie was restless, but getting back onto her was a huge mistake. I had fallen off and hit my head.

And out of all the people who came to look for me, it was Beck. I don't know what I'm supposed to feel for that. Should I feel appreciative that he found me? All I can think about right now is how he lied to me for the past month and tricked me into falling in love with him. Why would he do that?

Dad leaves to get the doctor, leaving Mum alone with me.

"Mum, I feel like a fool," I tell her.

Mum pats my head gently. "Oh, Emma. You aren't a fool."

"Yes, I am. I should have paid attention to the trials, then I would have known that the guy Annie hired as a farmhand was the guy who killed Dean. I should have listened to you."

Mum gives me a small smile. "It's okay, sweetie. You know who he really is now, and you don't have to talk to him if you don't want to."

I nod slowly. All I want is for Beck to disappear from my life again. I want to forget that I have fallen in love with him. He shouldn't be the person I fall in love with, not after what he did. He says he has changed since going to jail, it makes no difference. I can't be with someone who killed my boyfriend, and almost killed me also.

The doctor came in to check on me, explaining that I have a concussion from my fall. The whole time he speaks, all I can think about is Beck. My head injury is minor, but I'll be staying overnight for observation. I should take it easy, and I need plenty of rest before I'll be alright again in the next few days. What if I go back to Annie's, and Beck's still there? I can't bear to see him right now.

I don't want to see him for the rest of my life.

Chapter 28

Beck

It's all over. After twenty-three years and a filed police report, we are finally safe.

After the police finish talking with Mum and Chandler, Chandler leaves to give Mum and me some privacy. He promises to call me later and to let me know if I ned anything.

I sit down next to Mum's bed. "How are you feeling, Mum?"

"Tired," she says. "The painkillers I was given are making me drowsy."

"I can leave and let you rest."

She shakes her head. "No, it's okay. You can stay here with me."

"I'm really glad you are okay, Mum. When you called me, I was so worried about what Dad was doing to you."

She curls her lips into a small smile. "I'm fine, sweetie."

"I wish we reported Dad a long time ago. This has gone on for far too long."

Mum sits there in silence for a moment. "I know it has, Beck. And I'm sorry I have put you through all of this abuse for so long. I shouldn't have done that. It's just I was worried I would never be able to find us a safe place. I was worried he would find us if we ever left him. And the last thing I wanted was for you to be taken away. If I had lost you, I wouldn't know what I would have done with my life."

I carefully wrap my arms around and hug her. "It's okay, Mum. Everything is going to be okay now."

Mum pulls away from me. "Enough with what happened. Tell me, how was the wedding?"

The wedding. It's the last thing I want to talk about, but I tell her everything.

"I messed up, Mum. I know I should have told Emma the truth, but I didn't know how to. I knew if I told her, there was a chance she will turn around and hate me, and that's exactly what she has done. She said she was going to make Annie fire me. If Annie does, I don't know what I'm going to do next. Annie gave me a chance. What if I don't get another chance somewhere else?"

Mum pats her good hand on my arm. "Everything is going to be alright, Beck. I'm sure Annie won't fire you. Maybe let Emma calm down. Remember, this is like a bombshell to her. She might need some time to think. Maybe the two of you will be able to talk about what happened."

I shake my head. "I don't think she's going to talk to me. She has pretty much made it clear that she hates me."

"I'm sure she doesn't hate you."

I want to believe Mum, but I saw the way Emma looked at me with all the hurt and anger in her eyes. She isn't going to be forgiving. And that's all on me for never telling the truth to her since she told me about Dean. I should have confessed everything there. I let this romance blossom between us, hiding the biggest, dark secret of my life from her. But it doesn't matter now that

I didn't tell her. I have lost her. Going to the wedding was a big mistake.

I leave Mum, letting her rest and promising to come back tomorrow.

Emma is somewhere in this hospital, and I wonder if she has woken up yet. Would she let me see her? Probably not, but I want her to know how much I deeply care about her one last time.

I head down to the reception and ask for Emma's room. The receptionist directs me to where I need to go, and I follow the directions to her room.

My mind fills up with a hundred million things I want to say to her, but I don't know exactly what will happen when I see her. I find her room, and when I take taking a peek inside, my heart dances when I see that she is awake. But I can't go in. Her parents are in there, and I know if I try to step into this room, her father is going to stop me from going anywhere near his daughter.

Before anyone sees me, I quickly get out of the ward. Emma is okay, and I hope she will allow me to talk with her like my mother said she might one day.

But if Emma doesn't forgive me for what I did, I don't know how I'll be able to live without her.

It's late, and I don't want Chandler to have to drive me all the way to Maisy Grove, so I stay with him and Lisa tonight.

"Let me know or Chandler if you need anything," Lisa tells me after finishing setting up the guest room.

I smile at her. "Thanks, Lisa."

"Chandler and I are going to watch a movie. You're welcome to join us."

"Thanks, but I'm really tired. I'm just going to go to bed."

Lisa nods. "Sure." She turns to leave but then turns back to me. "Chandler told me what happened with you and Emma. I'm really sorry. I hope both of you can work something out. She seems like a nice person, and even though you have an unfortunate past, I think you're both perfect for each other."

Lisa walks out of the room and closes the door behind her.

I sit down on the bed and pull out my phone, glancing through the gallery of the photos I had taken of Emma and me together. There's one I had taken of her grooming Blondie, laughing happily. There's another one we had taken down at the river, cuddling up together. I recall the first day I arrived at the farm, how she never seemed happy. And then she started hanging around me, and something changed. She became a whole different person, happy, enjoying life.

And now, I wonder if I'm ever going to see that side of Emma again.

I decide to check in on Annie and let her know I'm staying with Chandler. I'm not even sure how long I'll be here, or how long Mum is going to be in the hospital. The doctor has to wait for the swelling to go down before they can put a cast on Mum's arm. And I'm not sure if I'll be needed at the police station, but I'm pretty sure the police have all of the information they need to lock away my dad for a long time.

"Take your time, Beck," Annie assures me. "If you need a couple of days to stay with your friend, it's fine. And if your mother needs a safe place to stay, she is welcome to stay here."

"Thanks, Annie. Have you heard anything about Emma?" I leave out the part where I tried to see her.

"I spoke with her mother a while ago. Emma has woken up. She has a mild concussion and is staying overnight at the hospital and will be allowed to come home tomorrow. She may be staying with her parents for a few days before she comes back to the farm."

"I'm glad she's alright. If you talk to her, can you tell Emma that I'm thinking about her."

"I will."

"And Annie, if you need any help on the farm, call me. I can come home and help you around."

"I will be alright, Beck. You stay with your mother. I have Darcy and Roxanne to help me out with anything."

"Alright. See you soon, Annie."

I hang up the phone and lie down on the bed, staring up at the ceiling and thinking about Emma. I think about what I could say to her the next time I see her. The question is, will she allow me to see her the next time, or would she still be mad at me?

I decide to call Emma. I need to hear her voice before I fall asleep. I want her to know how deeply sorry I am and how I care so much about her.

I listen to the phone ring, hoping she has her phone on her and she's able to talk.

"Hi, you have reached Emma. I'm not able to take your call right now, but please leave me a message, and I will return your call as soon as I can."

I don't leave a message. I hang up and call her again. Maybe she'll answer the second time. But no such luck. Her voicemail plays again.

This time, I leave a message. "Hey, Emma. It's me, Beck. Look, I know you don't want to talk to me right now, and I totally understand if you don't. But I just want to say I'm sorry, and that I hope you're alright. I hope to chat with you soon."

I hang up, and stare at my phone for a long time, hoping Emma hears my message and returns the call. But my phone remains silent. My heart crumbles. How did I stuff everything up between us? Is there a way for me to repair everything?

Chapter 29

Emma

Daniel and Kristy don't find out about my accident until their wedding is over. They come by the next morning to see how I am, unhappy that my parents didn't inform them what had happened. But I'm glad my parents didn't, because I didn't want to be the reason for ruining their wedding day. It's bad enough that I had brought Beck along, and everything could have been a lot worse if Daniel had beaten him up.

When the doctor discharges me later that afternoon, and I don't go back to Annie's, I decide to spend a few days at my parents' house. Hopefully by the time I'm ready to head back home, Beck has packed up and left. I don't care where he goes, just as long as he isn't near me. He has tried to call me a few times, but I refused to answer. He even left me a voice message, asking me how I was and that he is sorry about everything. Is he sorry, though?

"Do you need me to drive over to Annie's and grab anything you might need?" Mum asks as she walks me to my old bedroom, which is now a guest bedroom.

I shake my head, sitting down on the bed. "It's fine, Mum. I'll only be here for a few days."

Mum gives me a warm smile. "Alright. Well, I will let you settle in. Let me know if you need anything."

Mum leaves, closing the door behind her.

When she's gone, I pull out my phone and open my gallery. I scroll down until I come to the very last photo I had ever taken of Dean and me. It was on the night of our formal. Mum had taken the photo of us together out on the patio. I smile at the picture, remembering this night all too well. My back rests against Dean's torso, and his arms are wrapped around my waist as we pose for the photo, smiling. There's another one of us in the same position but while laughing. How did the best night of my life that I had looked forward to all through high school turn into the most tragic day of my life?

Not thinking about Beck is harder than I thought it would be. Every time I think of what he did to Dean and me, all I want to do is scream. But then I think about the time we had been spending together, how he made me happy and had helped me to move on from Dean's death. It's like my brain is trying to pick out the good things about him and not allow me to be angry with what he did. It's stupid really, because as much as I had fallen for him, I couldn't think about being with him. He killed my boyfriend and could have potentially killed me too, but somehow I survived the accident. I don't care if Beck has changed in the last two years. I can never forgive him for what he did.

Katie and Sammy had called me a few times, wanting to see how I am, but I hardly spoke to them. Just a quick hello, and yes, I'm fine, before hanging up the phone. Rude, yeah, but I knew if I kept talking to them, the conversation would lead to Beck, and I didn't want to talk about him. It's bad enough that I already feel like a total fool for falling for him and then suggesting he come to my brother's wedding.

I do talk to Annie, though. She wants to see how I'm doing and know how long I'm planning to stay with my parents. And though I hate saying his name, as saying his name is like poison on the tip of my tongue, I ask her if Beck is still there. She explains to me that something happened with his parents and that his mother is in the hospital and his father has been arrested. He is staying with his friend for a few days until his mother is discharged.

There's a part of my heart that goes out to Beck and wants to call him up, then I remind myself that I'm mad at him. Even if I call to see how his mum is doing, he will then try to turn the conversation towards us, trying to apologise to me, and I just can't accept his apology. I also talk with my boss, who gives me the week off to rest up before I come back to work.

I spend the next few days throwing myself into baking. An apple pie for dinner, one for Sammy and Katie, and even one waiting for when Daniel and Kristy get back from their honeymoon.

On Friday, I decide to head back to Annie's. The markets are tomorrow, and she is going to need help. I drive nervously up her gravel driveway, unsure what to expect if I were to see Beck. Has he returned yet or is he still with his friend? I hope he is still with his friend.

Darcy and Roxanne come out of the stables as soon as I get out of my car.

"Hey, Emma," Darcy says as she and Roxanne walks over to me. "Annie told us what happened. How are you?"

I give them a small smile. "I'm feeling good, thank you."

After a small exchange, Darcy and Roxanne go back to work. From the car, I take out the apple pie I made yesterday to bring home for Annie. She's over near the goat pen, feeding them. As I approach the pen, all I can think of is the struggle Beck had getting into the pen, all because Buckley disliked him. The thought almost makes me laugh, but then I remind myself not to think of Beck. I need to forget about him.

But how do you forget the person you have fallen so hard for?

"Hey, Annie."

Annie looks up at me and smiles. She walks over to me, and some of the goats follow her, along with Buckley.

"It's so good to see you," she says, giving me a one-arm hug while she holds onto the bucket. The goats try to stick their heads inside, and Buckley tries to knock it out of her hand. Annie pulls away from me and rests the bucket on top of the fence so the goats can't get to it. "How are you doing?"

"I'm good, thanks. It was nice spending some time with my parents."

"That's good to hear."

I hold up the pie. "I made an apple pie for dessert later."

"Thank you, dear. Why don't you bring that inside? I'd better finish feeding these goats."

"I'm sorry I haven't been around for the whole week. You have been okay with working around the farm?"

Annie nods. "Yes, I have been. My son came over to help me around the farm while you and Beck took the week off. Darcy and Roxanne helped with the horses and the stable."

"Do you need help with anything today?"

Annie shakes her head. "I'm pretty much done. You rest up. Maybe you would like to go and see Blondie, maybe take her for a ride? She has been worried about you."

I head inside, placing the pie in the fridge before heading to the stables. I look around for Darcy and Roxanne, hoping they don't come and ask me questions about what happened or about Beck. They don't need to know what went on between Beck and me Telling them will mean having to tell them about Dean, and I don't want to talk about him to them.

Not seeing the girls anywhere, I head straight to Blondie's stall. She's eating hay, but as soon as she sees me standing at the stall, she walks over to me, her tail swinging freely.

"Hey, girl." I pat her snout. "How are you doing? Miss me?"

Blondie neighs in answer.

I wrap my arms around her neck and rest my head against hers. "I miss you, too. I hope I didn't spook you too much when I fell off." I rub Blondie's neck. "I'm sorry I took you out when a storm was coming. I know the thunder scares you. I just needed to get away."

Blondie nibbles my hair. I laugh and move away.

"I feel so stupid, Blondie. How could I let myself fall for Beck? I mean, it was obvious when he couldn't fully tell me what happened, only telling me he had been drink driving and went to jail. I should have known he was the one who crashed into Dean and me. I can't love someone like that."

"Loving someone despite them doing something horrible to us is never easy." I turn to see Annie walking into the stable. "Sometimes we fall for someone we know we shouldn't."

"But Annie, I can't fall for someone like Beck."

Annie stands at the stall next to me. Raven pokes his head out of the stall. Annie scratches him behind the ear. "Why not?"

I give Annie a look that says she should already know the answer. "He killed my boyfriend. He could have potentially killed me too."

"Beck hasn't explained everything to me yet, but I'm sure he regrets everything that he has done and is trying to make things right."

I shake my head. Even if this is what Beck is trying to do, he can never make things right. How can you, after taking away someone's life, act like everything is okay with that person's partner? What is Beck trying to prove by getting with me? For the past two years, I have struggled with moving on from Dean's death. Since meeting Beck, I really thought I had found a reason to move on with my life. But now, knowing Beck is the reason why Dean isn't here, I'm not sure if I could move on after all.

"Things will never be the same," I say, "no matter how much Beck wants to change it."

I wait for Annie to say something wise like she always does, but this time she doesn't. She has her eyes on Raven, scratching behind his ears.

She then moves away from him, turning to me. "Anyway, I just came to say that Roxanne and Darcy have finished cleaning the stables for the day. If you'd like, you can take Blondie out for a ride. I'm going to head inside and get dinner started. Dinner should be ready by the time you get back."

I smile at her. "Alright, Annie."

Annie returns the smile. "It's great to have you back, Emma. I'm glad you're alright."

"I am, too."

Annie walks away, heading back towards the house. I turn to Blondie.

"Do you want to go for a ride down to the river?" I ask her.

Blondie neighs and I give her another hug before heading to the tack room to grab her saddle and bridle.

Chapter 30

Beck

The next few days go by slowly.

Mum has been discharged from the hospital after two days, and Chandler and Lisa have continued to allow us to stay with them. We could have gone back to our house, but I never want to set foot in that place again.

Dad hasn't been granted bail, and I'm thankful for that. If he were allowed out, I can guarantee he would come after Mum and me, probably kill us for real for calling the police.

On Friday afternoon, Annie calls me up, inviting me over for dinner. She says there's something she needs to discuss with me. The moment she says it, my stomach twists into knots, knowing that this is it. She's going to fire me. I agree to come.

Chandler drives me back to Annie's. I thank him for the lift and promise to call him later.

As he heads back down the driveway, I glance around the farm, unsure if I will ever see this place again. Emma's car is parked next to Annie's, so I know she's here, and I wonder where she is and if I'll see her. I'm not even sure what I'll do if I see her again. She hasn't responded to my message, and it's most likely she isn't going to. She clearly wants nothing to do with me, and I don't blame her. I probably wouldn't want anything to do with myself either.

I glance over at the guest house, wondering if Emma's inside.

When I walk up the front steps of Annie's house and knock on the door, I hear Jessie's barks from the inside. The door opens within a few minutes with Annie standing on the other side in an apron.

"I'm so glad you could come, Beck."

Jessie runs out the door the moment it opens and jumps on me, placing her front paws on my thighs. I scratch behind her ears, greeting her before she's told by Annie to get down. Annie moves aside for me, and I enter the house.

"How's your mother doing?" Annie asks.

"She is good. We're currently staying with my friend. I'm not sure when to go back to the house."

Annie closes the door. "What's happening with your father?"

"He is currently in custody. He should have court sometime next week."

"I'm glad your mother is alright. Remember, you're both welcome to stay here."

The thought of it makes my stomach twist. Why is Annie being so nice to me?

I thank her for her offer. I doubt she genuinely wants to house my mother and me.

Annie leads me to the kitchen that smells of lamb.

"How's Emma?" I ask, sitting at the table. Jessie sits next to me.

"Emma is doing okay," Annie answers. She turns to me. "I haven't told her you're coming for dinner today because I know she will refuse to join. Are you comfortable with her joining us?"

I nod. "Of course I am." Though, I'm not sure how I'm going to react when I see her.

The oven timer goes off, and Annie puts on her mitts to check on her trays of roast vegetables and lamb before setting the timer for another few minutes.

Annie then turns to me, taking off her mitts. "Emma hasn't exactly explained to me everything that has happened between the two of you. All she has told me is that you're the one who caused the accident that killed her boyfriend,"

I bow my head in shame, not looking at Annie. Now it's my turn to explain everything to Annie. I scratch Jessie behind her ears before forcing myself to look up at Annie, who is watching me carefully. Will she take back her offer once I tell her the rest of what happened?

I explain to Annie what happened that night and everything that has happened since. I can see the headlights of Dean's car clear in my mind. I had closed my eyes for a second, and when I opened them, there was barely any time to swerve to the other side. I can't forget the sound of the deafening crunch of our vehicles colliding and the shattering of the impact. My memory of the accident is in fragments of what happened in the aftermath. I don't remember if I knew what I had done until I woke up in the hospital. As soon as the officers informed me what happened, I realised what I did. I took a life because of my decision. It was something I knew I could never take back. I tell Annie how I didn't know Emma was the person who was also in the car when I started here, and how I wasn't sure how I was supposed to tell her when I knew she was going to hate me. Annie listens carefully as I talk, not saying a word until I finish.

"I can see why Emma is upset," she says.

"Are you upset with me?" I ask her. "Do you hate me also?"

Annie shakes her head. "No, Beck. I don't hate you, and I'm not upset. It's not my place to judge you for what you did in the past. But I can see how much you've changed and how much you want to change your life so you don't go back to being the person you were."

I sigh with relief, a weight lifting from my shoulders I didn't know was weighing me down.

"It's going to take Emma a long time to forgive you for what happened," Annie goes on. "What you did, it isn't an easy thing for someone to forgive."

"I know," I answer. "I wish there was a way to make it up to her, but I don't think I ever could."

"All you can do right now is give her space. When she is ready, let her be the one to approach you."

The oven timer goes off once more, and Annie checks the lamb before switching the oven off.

"Are you sure you want me here for dinner?" I double-check. "Emma isn't going to be pleased to see me. And like you said, she might refuse to join us when she knows I was here."

Annie sets the tray on the counter and turns to me. "I'm aware of what's going to happen once Emma walks in. But I need the both of you here because there's something I need to discuss with you."

I swallow. This is it. Annie is going to be telling me that my stay here is over, that she will be taking Emma's side because it's all for the best for everyone that I'm not here. "Are you letting me go?"

Annie shakes her head. "No, I'm not doing that. I just need you both to get along when I tell you."

I nod. "I can do that."

"I know you can, Beck. But it's Emma I'm worried about."

"It's going to be alright, Annie. Yes, Emma and I might argue, but we'll listen to what you have to say."

Annie smiles. "Thank you, Beck. Now, why don't you set the table, and I'll serve up this food?"

I do what Annie asks me, and as I set the table, I think about Emma, and wonder what's going to happen during this dinner. How is she going to react when she sees me?

After another ten minutes, the food is ready, and the front door squeaks open. I hold my breath. Emma walks in and stops when she sees me. She looks between me and Annie before her eyes are fully set and narrowed on me.

"What are you doing here?" she asks. "I hope you're here to pack your bags."

Annie spins around. "No, he is here for dinner. I've invited him to sit with us this evening."

"Well, I'll come back later. I don't want to sit at the same table as *him*," she says the last word like it's poison.

Emma turns to leave, but Annie stops her before she can.

"I know you don't want to be in the same room as Beck right now, but I need you to. There's something I need to tell you both, and I need you both to listen. So please, Emma. Sit down and eat with us."

Emma narrows her eyes once more before listening to Annie and taking a seat across from me.

Annie places the plates down in front of us before sitting down in between us. We thank her for the meal and eat in silence.

"I know things aren't right between the both of you, but I really needed you both here today," Annie breaks the silence. "I'm selling up, and I'm going to be moving in with my son."

Emma and I stare at her in silence, taking in her news.

"What do you mean you're selling this place?" Emma speaks first. "You can't sell it!"

"I'm seventy years old, and I feel it's time for me to let this farm go," Annie explains. "I have been holding onto this place for a long time since my husband passed away, but I can't keep running this farm on my own. It's tiring for me even though I know I have people to help me to run it."

"You could have told us sooner, Annie," I say. "We could have done more around the farm to help you out."

Annie smiles. "I know, Beck. And you all do a good job at helping me. I really appreciate it."

"Wait, why is it just Beck and I here?" Emma says. "Why isn't Darcy and Roxanne also here? Or have you already broken the news to them?"

Annie shakes her head. "I haven't told them anything yet. No, I invited you both to dinner despite your differences to tell you I want to hand over this farm over to you, Emma. Beck, I would like you to help Emma run the property."

Emma and I turn our gazes from Annie to each other. Emma and I to take over this farm? It's a nice offer, but I doubt Emma and I could take ownership together. Not when she despises me.

"Annie, there is no way Beck or I could afford to buy this place from you," Emma says.

"Yes, I'm aware of that," Annie nods. "Which is why instead of selling it to you, I'm transferring the property over to you. Of course, there will be a payment, and I understand if you can't pay right now, but I'm willing to come up with a payment agreement."

Emma and I glance over at each other again before turning back to Annie. It honestly feels like a big joke, but Annie looks serious. She darts her eyes between us, waiting for us to say something. How could she simply hand the property over to us? Selling it to someone who can afford it would be so much better for her.

"Annie, this is a nice offer, but why do you want to transfer it over to us?" I ask. "Wouldn't it be better to just sell it?"

Annie takes a sip of her drink, nodding before answering again. "You're right. I should sell it. Even my son suggested I sell the property. He has been wanting me to sell this place since my husband passed away, thought the property would be too big to run on my own. But I have had so many amazing people help me run it. Beck, Emma, I have been observing the two of you for the past few weeks. Yes, I could sell this place, but I don't want to hand the property over to just anybody. I see the love you both have for this place and how you treat the animals. I know you both will take good care of it."

She turns to Emma. "I know how everything hasn't been great for you in the last few years, Emma. But since coming here, you have picked yourself up. I enjoy your help around the farm and helping me at the farmer's market I also remember when you mentioned that we should consider having a trail ride with the horses down to the river. I think with you owning the farm, you can go ahead and offer that to people. It will be great for the horses to go on long walks rather than only being used for riding lessons. My late husband and I used to take the horses on long walks all the time, but now I don't have the time to do that as much as I want to."

I expect Emma to say something, but instead, she sits there, speechless.

Annie turns to me next. "And Beck, I understand you have recently gotten out of jail and you're trying to prove you aren't the person who you used to be. I know you also weren't expecting to cross paths with Emma, and that you want to make the past right. I know I haven't known you for long, but I see potential in you as you set your path straight."

I look over at Emma, waiting for her to say some kind of smart remark. She would have something to say about what I did to Dean. Annie is right. I do want to try to make the past right. I no longer want to be the alcoholic I was when I was trying to escape my problems. With Dad now in custody, and his guilty charge pending, I'm determined to give myself a better life not only for me, but for my mother as well.

But still speechless from Annie's offer, Emma continues to sit there in silence.

I turn my attention back to Annie.

"You have been taking good care of the animals here," Annie goes on, "and I really appreciate your help. You have also brought Emma out of her shell. Before you came, she was never happy, and it was hard to even get one smile out of her. I know things have taken a turn for both of you, but I believe you will sort things out. I believe in both of you. And Beck, my offer still stands. Your mother is welcome to stay here for as long as she needs. This will be a great place for her to start over."

I smile at her. "Thank you, Annie. I really appreciate it."

Annie returns the smile before looking between the both of us. "So, what do you guys say? Is this something you would like?"

I'm about to open my mouth to answer. This is an incredible offer Annie was giving the both of us. And the idea of Mum and I starting over here sounds great. Dad would never find us here if he ever gets out. But before I get the chance to answer, Emma speaks up.

"I need to think about this, Annie," she says. "This a great offer, but I don't think it's a good idea for Beck and me to be living here together. I'm not sure if I also want to run this place on my own."

Annie nods. "Of course. Take your time thinking about it. I will give you both until Sunday to give me an answer."

Emma stands up from the chair, her dinner barely touched. "Thank you, Annie, for this meal."

She leaves the room and heads to the front door.

I follow her out.

"Beck, do not follow me," Emma says without even turning back to see that I am. "I don't want to talk to you right now."

"And why don't you want to talk to me right now?" I ask her.

She stops a few metres from the front steps and turns to me, her eyes teary with a mix of anger. "Why? Are you stupid or something? I don't want to talk to you because you lied to me, Beck. You couldn't even tell me you were the guy who killed Dean! How do you expect me to react to you? How do you expect me to fall in love with you after what you did to him? I can't be with someone who killed him."

I nod, because how could I expect her to forgive me for what I had done?

"Hear me out, Emma. I'm sorry for what I did. I know it wasn't right for me to get behind the wheel while intoxicated. It was wrong for me to do so. If I could go back to that day, I would. I would change everything. I would have called a taxi to get me home. I should have never done that. I'm an idiot for doing that. I know my apology won't bring Dean back. Every day, I live with so much regret over it all. Every decision and choice I've ever made. But there is one thing I don't regret, and that's falling for you."

Emma shakes her head. "You can't say you've fallen for me, Beck. Not after what you did. I can't be with you. And even if Annie thinks we're great together and wants us to take over this farm, I don't want to live here with you."

Her words are like a knife in my heart. This is exactly how I'd imagined she'd react. She is never going to forgive me, and I'm sure what I'm supposed to do with my life, knowing that I'll never get to be with her again.

"Look, I know every single apology I make will never make up for what I did," I say. "But I'm really sorry, Emma, and I wish I could make it up to you. When I first learned who you were, I knew I should have told you who I was. But I was a coward and didn't know how to tell you. I was falling for you, and I didn't want to lose you."

Emma crosses her arms across her chest. "You're right. You can make as many apologies as you want, and it will never make up for what you did. I honestly really thought I was finally moving on from Dean's death after meeting you. Now, I don't even know what I'm doing. I feel like I'm living the accident all over again, and now Annie has just decided that she wants to hand this property over to both of us. Maybe if no one opened my eyes to who you really were, I would jump at this opportunity, but I can't do that anymore. I can't be with you, Beck."

The knife has completely torn and cut out my heart.

"Please, Emma. Just give me another chance to make everything right."

Emma shakes her head. "I can't give you another chance. There is nothing to make right. What's done will forever be done. Dean is dead, and giving you a second chance would be like saying what you did is okay."

I shake my head. "No, that's not how it needs to be, Emma. There must be some kind of reason as to why the two of us are here together. We have the chance to move on from the past together. Let me show you I can make everything right."

Emma stares at me for a very long time before saying, "No. There isn't a reason as to why we're here together. It's just bringing back memories I don't want to remember. Look, just do me a favour, Beck, and get out of my life. I don't want to ever see you again."

Without another word, she walks off, and all I can do is hopelessly watch. If only I could get her to realise that there is some kind of reason why we needed to be together. There has to be.

I imagine running up to her, kissing her, hoping it will get her to change her mind and remember her love for me. But in reality, it won't end well. I watch her slam the door of the guest house before I head back inside, utterly torn.

Annie is still sitting at the table, her food now cold on her plate. I feel bad she spent so much time putting this dinner together for none of us to be in the mood to eat.

"She still doesn't want to talk to you?" Annie guesses.

I walk over to the table and lean on a chair. "Thank you for dinner, Annie. I'm sorry you invited us here in hopes that we would accept your offer, which sounds really good, but I'm not sure how it's going to work when Emma hates my guts."

Annie nods. "I know. Give her time, Beck. She just needs her space."

"For how long is she going to need her space, though? She pretty much made it clear she doesn't want to see me ever again."

"From the way I have observed the both of you the last month, I can see the love you have for each other. I know you have this unforgivable past, and I know it will take time for you to move on from this and make this relationship work. But since you arrived here, Beck, I have never seen Emma so happy. She came here as a broken eighteen-year-old, unsure of what she wanted to do with her life after her boyfriend died. She was fairly quiet, hardly spoke to anyone, especially not to her friends or family. Her brother often came around to check in on her, but she pretty much shut herself out from the world. And then you came around and brought a smile to her face."

I'm the one who's responsible for breaking Emma. She's right, I don't deserve a second chance, even if I'm the person who also made her happy again.

"Emma has made it pretty clear she doesn't want to see me ever again," I say. "So, I might just call my friend to come pick me up and get me out of here."

I pull out my phone, but before I get a chance to call up Chandler, Annie speaks.

"Why don't you stay the night here and leave in the morning?"

"No, I really think I need to leave."

Annie shakes her head. "No. This is my house, Beck. I want you to stay for the night. I don't care what Emma says."

I nod. "Okay. But tomorrow morning, I'll be leaving."

I turn to leave, but before I do, I ask, "Annie, you haven't known me for long. How can you trust me to run this farm with Emma?"

She smiles at me. "Everyone deserves a second chance. I see how you have changed Emma's life since being here. I believe being on this farm has given you a second chance, and I know when Emma feels like she can forgive you, maybe she will give you one too."

"What if she chooses to never forgive me?" My heart aches at the thought. "She even said she won't."

"Then at least you know you tried to make things right. We all make mistakes, but it's up to us to change it."

Chapter 31

Emma

Why is moving on the hardest thing? Why can't things go back to being perfect like the way it was so you never have to move on with your life? If Dean were here, I would be with him. I probably wouldn't be living here on Annie's farm, though it would be nice to live here with Dean. He would enjoy it here. By now, I'm sure we would have settled into our own place. We could be engaged or perhaps already married. Instead, I'm living in a town that isn't my own, on a faraway farm with no one I knew, all to escape the pain that Beck caused. Then, for the first and only time I thought I found a way to move on, it turns out to be with the man who claimed Dean's life. He almost claimed mine, and for years I've wondered and am still trying to figure out why. Why didn't I die with Dean?

Because then you wouldn't have met Beck, a little voice in the back of my mind says.

How could someone like Beck, who took away the most important person in my life, make me feel so good about myself? From the moment I saw him to the times we hung out and then to our first kiss together, how is it possible to fall in love with someone who took away the person you had loved?

As I walked through the guest house, everything holds some kind of memory of Beck. The couch where he sat after Buckley rammed him, the coffee table I sat on to help him with the ice pack before we made out. The kitchen where we made hot chocolate and decided at that moment how much we meant to each other. And the one memory I still think about is when Beck carried me to my bed. The feeling of his skin on mine as we made love for the first time. It isn't fair.

Could I even be happy with Beck knowing what he had done?

I'm still in love with him, no matter how much I tell myself I'm not, but he's someone I can't be with. My heart breaks at the sight of him. It shouldn't do that when you're in love with someone.

I leave the guest house. I can't be in there at the moment. Annie's house is dark, so she is probably asleep, and I don't see Beck anywhere. Taking a walk down to the river isn't a good idea right now, so I head to the barn. The horses are sound asleep, and I creep through the barn, hoping not to wake any of them. I walk into the tack room and sit down on a stool.

I take out my phone and stare at it for a moment, trying to decide who to call. Maybe Mum. Could she help me even though I haven't spoken to her in so long? But talking to her about Beck isn't a good idea. Could she even understand my feelings right now? I haven't spoken to her about Beck the whole week I stayed with my parents. He was a forbidden topic in the household after what he had put us through. I definitely can't talk to my friends about him. Straight out, they will tell me I shouldn't see him. I'm not even sure if I could tell anyone about Annie's offer because straight away, they would tell me not to live here if Beck is going to. I honestly don't even know if I want to take on the farm regardless of him. But Annie was right about one thing, and that is about the trail riding with the horses. But did I want to open that up to the public and do it without Annie's help?

The only person I could think of talking to about Beck is Kristy.

She answers the phone after a few rings. "Hey, Emma. How are you doing?"

I force myself to smile even though Kristy can't see me through the phone. "I'm good, thanks. How's the honeymoon?"

I can hear the television in the background, and I feel horrible for calling her up when probably all she wants is to be alone with my brother.

"It's great down here," Kristy says. "We'll be coming home over the weekend, and I honestly don't want to leave."

"That's good. I'm glad you are having fun. Hey, Kristy, I'm sorry to bother you, but I was wondering if it's okay that I can talk to you?"

"Sure. Just give me a second." I hear her talking to my brother, telling him she's going outside for some girl talk. Daniel says okay, and I hear some shuffling and a sliding door. "What do you want to talk about?"

I inhale a deep breath, ready to tell Kristy everything. "I don't know who I should talk to. After Sunday, I feel like everyone will judge me and tell me to stay away from Beck. I know I should stay away from him, and I don't want to see him again, but I'm in love with him, Kristy. I don't know what I should do. How do you love someone knowing they did something horrible to you?" I then tell her about Annie's offer, how she wants Beck and I to take over her property. There's so much going on in my life that I just don't know what I should be doing.

Kristy is silent on the other end for a moment before speaking. "I'm not sure what I can really say to you, Emma. All I know is that you aren't stupid for falling for Beck. These kinds of things happen. We fall for people we think we'd never fall for. It's just something we do. Like your brain knows something that your heart probably doesn't."

I think about what Annie said to me earlier in the stables.

"Loving someone despite them doing something horrible to us is never easy. Sometimes we fall for someone we know we shouldn't."

"Annie reckons Beck is trying to make up for who he once was. He was an alcoholic because of his dad, but there is no way he can make up to me for what he did to Dean."

"Annie sounds like a wise person. I'll have to come visit someday and meet her."

I smile. "Annie is a lovely person. She has helped me through a lot with Dean."

"That's great, Emma. Has Beck ever tried to apologise to you about everything that happened?"

"He has, but I don't want to hear it. Nothing he says can take away the pain or heal the betrayal. And I feel like I'm betraying Dean for being with the person who killed him."

"Don't feel like you are betraying Dean, Emma. I'm sure Dean is really happy you've found someone."

"Yes, but he wouldn't want me to fall in love with the killer."

"No, he wouldn't. Have you tried talking with Beck?"

"He has tried to talk with me, but I don't want to talk with him."

"You should sit down and talk with him. I know what he did was horrible, but it was an accident. Definitely one that could have been avoided, but it happened, and I'm sure spending time in jail has helped see a new perspective. Has he been trying to make new changes in his life?"

I nod. "Yeah, he stopped drinking. He said he never wanted to touch alcohol ever again after what happened."

"See, Emma. He is trying to change his ways so he doesn't repeat his past actions. I know you say you can't forgive him for what he did to Dean, but you need to look at how Beck has become a new person. He has left his old self behind and is trying to make changes within his life. And his first priority should be making everything up to you. He knows what he did can't bring back Dean, but it sounds like he wants to do everything in his power to make sure you're happy. And since he started working at the farm, I never seen you happier, Emma."

Kristy and Annie had been saying similar things, which makes me confused more about my feelings because even if Beck is trying to make up for his past, falling for him is like betraying Dean. All I can think about is what he did, and there's no way I can ever let that go.

I thank Kristy for her advice, though I'm not sure if it helped at all.

I leave the stables and head back to the guest house.

I have some ingredients left to make an apple pie, and I decide to make another one. Maybe if I bake this pie, it will distract me from my problems and help me forget everything, even for a little while. Maybe it could help me decide what to do. Do I take up Annie's offer? And do I really want to have Beck in my life, or do I want to walk away from him for good?

Chapter 32

Emma

The pie doesn't help the cloud of thoughts covering my mind. So, after baking it, I decide to watch a movie with a slice and a cup of tea, hoping it would keep my thoughts occupied or at least help me come to a decision. But it doesn't. I don't know what I want. As I eat the slice of pie, I wonder for a moment what it would be like to take over the farm. What would I do? Maybe I could plant an apple orchard and bake fresh apple pies for customers when they came to visit the farm. I could still do riding lessons and offer the trail rides to people. Annie's property is huge, and it would be a shame if it were to go to waste.

All this is good and fun to think about, but would I be happy if I really were to run this place on my own? What would it be like if Beck was to live here with me?

The questions haunt me to the next morning, the voices in my head all talking loud and at once, whether they're my own conscience telling me what I should be doing or my heart, and I'm not sure which I should be listening to do.

I force myself out of bed because there is no use trying to sleep anymore. I go to the kitchen and make myself a cup of tea, hoping it will keep me alert. As I make it, I check my phone to find I have a text message from an unfamiliar number, sent to me last night. I must have missed it.

Hi Emma, it reads. **It's Chandler, Beck's friend.**

I pause from reading the message, wondering why Chandler would be messaging me. Beck probably told him to. He knows I won't listen to him, so he got someone else to speak to me, like that would even get me to listen. I look out the kitchen window and over at Annie's house, wondering if Beck was still here or if he has left already. Annie's truck is not here, but it's Saturday, so she has probably already left for the Farmer's Market. I'm surprised she didn't ask me to come along this morning, or maybe she just thought I might need time to myself, which honestly is what I really do need right now. Rain has started to fall, and I watch the drops fall from my window.

I turn back to the message.

I know you don't want to hear from Beck, and you probably wouldn't want to hear from me too, but please listen to me. I know what Beck did in the past to your bf, and I can tell you he is deeply sorry for what he did. As his friend, I can tell you he is trying to change to be a better person. That night when he was intoxicated, he was going through a lot of things with his father. He wasn't himself, and was suffering from depression, refusing to get help and thought alcohol was the only thing that could provide relief.

But that is in the past, and he is now trying to correct himself. Since he started working on the farm, he has never been happier with himself. Especially when he met you. Beck is in love with you, Emma. He never wanted to hurt you when he learned who you were. And I know forgiving him

for what he did isn't easy, but please. I beg you to forgive him. Give him a second chance to prove he isn't the person he was in the past.

The jug stops boiling, but I don't make a move to pour the water into my mug. I read the message over and over again, which only makes my unsettling thoughts worse than they were last night.

Forgive Beck and give him a second chance? How do I do that, knowing he lied to me about who he was?

I stroll through my phone and find the last picture Dean and I had taken at our school formal. We looked so happy, ready for what the future would bring for us after that night. We had graduated and were ready for our final school holidays, planning things we would do before we went back to do our final exams, and then we were to be done with the school year. We weren't planning to go to university, but we had planned to find work and then travel. I knew Dean was someone I was going to spend the rest of my life with. He made up my whole world.

But in the blink of an eye, Dean was gone. Forever eighteen. We weren't travelling the world, and we weren't going to spend the rest of our lives together. If I could go back to that night, perhaps Dean could have taken a different route, and he would still be here. But if we weren't on the same road as Beck, he could have changed someone else's life instead of mine. It wouldn't be fair to that person like it wasn't fair to me.

I know forgiving someone is something my parents have always taught me to do. But this, how do I forgive someone for taking away Dean's life? And the worst thing they can do is act like everything is okay and that they aren't the one responsible for his death. Then I think, maybe if I had known who he was at the time, Annie wouldn't have hired him to work on this farm.

But would you have been happy if you did know it was him? I ask myself. *He was the first person who made you happy since Dean died. He helped you move on, where you would probably still be miserable and feeling sorry for yourself. Without Beck, you would never have moved on.*

"What do I do, Dean?" I whisper. "How do I make the right decision?"

My question hangs in the air, never to be answered. Because the only person who can really answer it is me.

I hear the sound of a car pulling up outside. I look outside, thinking maybe Annie has returned, but it isn't hers. It's a black sedan that has pulled up outside her house. A man climbs out. It's Chandler. He walks up the front steps and knocks on the door. It opens, and Beck stands on the other side.

I turn back to my phone, rereading Chandler's text. *I know forgiving him for what he did isn't easy, but please. I beg you to forgive him. Give him a second chance to prove he isn't the person he was in the past.*

I replay everything from the moment I met Beck when he first started here to our first kiss to how he would listen carefully about Dean, finding ways to make me feel better and let go of the past and move on. I can still feel the way he touched me, the way he kissed me, making the butterflies dance like crazy in my stomach, bringing back the feelings I had felt with Dean. I truly never thought I would feel anything again with anyone since Dean's passing...

Why are you making me feel things that I shouldn't with you, Beck? I ask myself.

The answer is obvious. I'm still in love with Beck, no matter how much he hurt me. I am in love with him, even if it's wrong to love him after everything he has done. And I know no one is going to accept him. But what matters is how I feel, and I'm sure over time, my family and friends will see what I see in him.

I turn back to the window, looking over at the front veranda. The door opens where Chandler and Beck carry out boxes. He's leaving, just like I had asked him to.

Chandler opens the back boot to place Beck's belongings inside. Beck takes a look around before landing his eyes on the guest house. My heart jumps in my chest, and I wonder if he could see me through the window. Does he know I'm watching him?

I wait for him to raise his hand to wave or to walk over here to say goodbye one last time before he goes. Instead, he gets into the car.

That's when I turn from the window and race outside. Chandler reverses back and starts to turn around.

"Wait!" I yell, hoping the guys will hear me.

Chandler must have heard me, or at least seen me, because he stops with a jolt. I'm halfway there when Beck emerges from the car. He watches me before closing the door and sprints the rest of the way to me.

"Don't go," I say to him, puffing as I catch my breath. "I know last night I told you to leave and that I never wanted to see you again. But I realise that's not what I want."

Beck stares at me, searching my eyes for something I hope he can find. The rain is coming down hard, and I know I'm going to regret running out here barefoot as the rain turns the dirt to mud. But right now, I don't care about the rain. Beck is wearing a white shirt, and it clings to his torso, revealing his muscles underneath. I try not to focus on that as I stare back at him, unsure if I should keep talking or wait for him to say something back.

"What do you want, Emma?"

What do I want?

People say you'll never forget your first love. Beck had asked me if I thought I would fall in love again. I didn't think I could. Not without Dean. But Beck showed me it is possible.

"I want you, Beck. For these past few weeks, you made me feel things I never felt I would ever feel again. It has been so hard to move on from the accident and to let Dean go. I was afraid to let him go, afraid of forgetting him. And you're probably the last person on this earth I should ever fall in love with, especially after what you did. A few people have been telling me to forgive you and to give you a second chance. I don't know if I'm ready to do that because I'm still hurt that you never told me the truth."

Beck swallows, his Adam's apple bobbing. "I'm sorry. I should have told you from the start. But I was afraid of losing you because … I love you."

"I love you too, Beck. You've made me feel better than I have ever felt since losing Dean. I didn't think I could fall in love again. I don't know if I should even give you a second chance, but I want to. I want you to stay, Beck. I want you to stay in my life and promise me you won't ever leave me. It will take some time for me to trust you again, but I'm willing to start over."

A smile curls onto Beck's lips. He takes a step closer to me. "I promise you, Emma, that I won't leave. I promise you I will show you the person I'm trying to become and not the person I was two years ago. I know I can never make up for what I did to Dean, but I can promise you I will protect you."

Beck cups his hands on my jaw, leaning down towards me. I close the gap between us. As we kiss, I feel in my bones this is the right decision. From this moment, I know I can move on and start a new life with Beck. Dean will always be a part of my life, and there's nothing I can do to change the past. Giving Beck a second chance wasn't going to be easy, but I was willing to if it meant I was going to be happier when around him.

Beckett Owens may have been the person who destroyed my life, but he is also the person who is helping me to put it back together again.

Want more in *Maisy Grove Weddings*? Keep a look out for the next
book in the series:

The Art of Faking It

Coming soon

Before you go, if you enjoy this book, don't forget to leave a review.
Thank you so much for reading

Acknowledgments

You would think that by the time I get to my thirteenth book that the acknowledgments become easier to write. Truthfully, they don't. Each acknowledgment you write you keep thinking who on earth am I going to thank.

For the past five years I have been struggling with burnout. For a while I thought it was just a writing slump, but it was in fact burnout. I'm not sure what caused it, and it hung around for some quite time. I wrote on and off, trying to find my place with my writing. After a while, I found my place and I couldn't be happier.

I came up with this story from a prompt I found on the internet. I changed a bit of the prompt, but kept the whole idea of the car accident. Many of the characters in this story like Emma, her family, her friends and Annie were old characters of a middle grade series I wrote between my primary and high school days. Of course, that series will never be published, but it was fun to revisit these characters and creating something new. I absolutely enjoyed writing this book, even when it took me a while to write it on and off.

One person I would like to thank is Misty McPhail. Thank you, Misty, for sharing some tips on what could help me with writing again and escaped burnout. I played around with some ideas, and *The Art of Moving On* is what really stuck to me.

Thank you for Georgia of Pixel and Quill for putting together this amazing cover. You brought the vision to life, even when I had so much trouble trying to figure out what I wanted.

Thank you for the writing community who stuck by me when I was struggling with burnout. Thank you for helping me to get through it all and finding my place again.

And lastly, thank you to my editor Elena for helping me with this chaotic mess of a book and helping me to make the best version as I could.

About the Author

Jessica Madden was born and raised in Sydney, Australia. She began writing stories since the age of eight. When she was nine, she realised that she wanted to be a writer more than anything in the world. At twenty-three years old, Jessica published her first book *Right Here Waiting for You*. Writing about characters falling in love has always been her favourite thing to write about.

When she is not writing, Jessica is often daydreaming up new storylines, and can be found lost in reading a good book.

You can follow her on Instagram and X @JessicaCMadden

Also by Jessica Madden

<u>YOUNG ADULT FICTION</u>

Right Here Waiting For You
The Jet Lag Diaries
Silent Love
If You Had Stayed
Hating Jamie Jackson
This Song Is For You

Storm Chasers
Chasing the Storm
Chasing Tornadoes

I Wasn't Supposed To Fall For You
I Wasn't Supposed To Fall For You
It's All Because Of You

<u>NEW ADULT FICTION</u>

With You
One Whole Night with You
Every Moment with You